Love Is in the Air

Anji Nolan

CRIMSON ROMANCE

F+W Media, Inc.

This edition published by
Crimson Romance
an imprint of F+W Media, Inc.
10151 Carver Road, Suite 200
Blue Ash, Ohio 45242
www.crimsonromance.com

ISBN 10: 1-4405-7095-7
ISBN 13: 978-1-4405-7095-7
eISBN 10: 1-4405-7096-5
eISBN 13: 978-1-4405-7096-4

Acknowledgments

Thank you Captain Gene of *waterwaynet.com*, who proved to me that a fishing boat can really fly. To my aviation experts Captain Bron Ama, enjoy retirement B; Captain Keith Taylor, still out there in the wide blue yonder, and my long-suffering friends, who listen to my crazy stories on a daily basis.

CHAPTER ONE

Sergeant Jim Cromwell couldn't ignore the stunning female pilot walking towards the hotel. Her uniform fit perfectly on her tall, athletic body, and her captain's hat, set with the usual gold braid, highlighted her blonde hair. As he drew closer, her ice blue eyes connected with his, and she smiled. In that moment, he was so distracted that he misjudged the curb and lurched forward. As he reached out to brace for the fall, a bullet zipped by his head and hit the pilot in the shoulder. When the force spun her around, she collided with him, and a second bullet coursed across his arm.

People around them screamed and scattered, and Jim's cop instinct kicked in. As he and the pilot fell together, he rolled her behind the cover of a parked car. He pulled out his phone, called for backup, and drew his gun.

Rising tentatively above the car's hood, he saw a black Dodge Ram speeding down the road, and as it hung a fast right, he got a flash of Maine's loon plate. He was unable to make out the number.

Lowering himself back to the ground, he shielded the pilot. He couldn't imagine why anyone would want to shoot such a beautiful woman. What enemies could she possibly have? Or had the shooter been aiming for *him*? Since he was working on a drug case, he knew there was always the danger of retaliation. Had he unwittingly put her in the line of fire when he tripped over the curb?

"Don't worry," he said to her frightened eyes. "I'm a cop. You'll be all right."

She blinked slowly. "Did I get shot?"

"Yes, but it doesn't look serious. I'm going to move you a little. I need your hat to apply pressure to the wound."

She winced. "I certainly feel pressure."

Jim adjusted his position. "Lie still. An ambulance will be here soon." As he glanced around, he saw three other people on the ground. They didn't look wounded—just scared. "Everybody okay?" They replied in the affirmative. "You … red shirt, stay down, but scooch this way nearer the car." The woman moved in closer. She was sobbing. "Stay near me, ma'am. Help is on the way."

"Something doesn't feel right," said the pilot. She grimaced in pain, and her eyes closed.

"Hey, hey, hey," barked Jim. "Stay with me here. No sleeping on the job. Come on now, wake up. What's your name?"

"Sophie—Sophie Berg."

"Hi Sophie, I'm Jim Cromwell."

"One of our heroic boys in blue."

"Something like that."

"Something like what?" asked Sophie.

"I'm with the Royal Canadian Mounted Police."

Sophie smiled thinly. "A Mountie?"

"Yeah."

"That's precious. What are you doing … "

Jim shook her gently. "Sophie … "

"Uh?"

"Come on, stay awake. And you're a pilot … "

Sophie giggled, which made her cough. "What gave me away?"

"Sense of humor still good; you're going to be all right."

Sophie pointed to Jim's arm. "What about you? Seems I'm not the only one with a leak—you're shot too."

Sirens wailed in the background.

• • •

Maine Medical Center's emergency room was empty when Jim and Sophie arrived. A nurse immediately took her to the O.R., and Jim was hustled into a treatment cubicle. After the flesh wound on his arm had been dressed, he gave a report to one of his colleagues, pacing impatiently as he talked. Then his phone rang. It was the lead cop at the scene.

"Hi, Jim," Chip said. "A witness also reported seeing a black Dodge Ram leaving the scene, but she said it had Massachusetts plates."

"I saw the *loon*, Chip. Could it have different plates front and back?"

"Anything's possible. I'll check local surveillance cameras and those on the turnpike. How're you doing?"

"Flesh wound, no big deal."

"And the pilot?"

"Not sure yet. I'll talk to you later." Knowing the investigation was in good hands, Jim turned his attention to Sophie. He found the nurse's station. "So, nurse," he said. "How long will Ms. Berg be in the O.R.? Will it be okay if I wait and talk to her?"

"I don't see why not, though I'm not sure how long it will be. They need to take out the bullet and make sure she's stable. Then you can interrogate her all you want."

"That's not what I had in mind."

"Oh?"

"Why would I want to interrogate her?"

The nurse looked surprised. "You don't know who she is?"

"She's a pilot—Sophie Berg."

"Clearly you don't read." The nurse pulled a gossip magazine from beneath the desk. She flipped the pages and placed it open on the countertop. "See, Sophie Berg, private pilot to the stars. Saw a piece about her exploits on *TMZ*. She knows 'em all. Practically every week she's flying off with a famous somebody or other."

As Jim looked at the photos of a tall, athletic blonde with a radiant smile, he did a double take. She was in uniform with her hair in a French braid when she was shot and looked amazing.

But in the pictures, she wore a purple dress, accentuating her curves, with her hair cascading below her shoulders. The button down navy blue pilot wasn't even close to the stunning woman in the magazine. Jim smiled; he couldn't mistake her piercing blue eyes, though. How could the same woman appear so strikingly different?

Jim handed the magazine back to the nurse. "I still don't see where the interrogation comes in."

"Gosh, have you been under a rock," said the nurse. "Wait a sec." She left and returned with her iPad primed to a news story. The headline read, "Private Airlines: Taking up the Slack or a Way Out for Drug Kingpins?"

Jim quickly scanned the article, which sited Granola Aviation, the airline for whom Sophie worked, and other charter airlines as not only catering to the needs of the rich and famous, but also transporting drug lords and their cargo. It hypothesized that because of certain people's immunity as they crisscrossed the continent, a powder keg of resentment was about to explode among the cartels.

"I bet that's why she was shot," suggested the nurse. "She knows too much. It's all there in the article."

"You don't know that," said Jim.

The nurse smiled indulgently. "Not for sure. But I watch *CSI* and *Criminal Minds*. I know how it goes down."

Jim smiled and made a mental note of the article's web site. "Right, cop shows. Totally real life. So when will I be able to see her?"

"Let me check what's going on. Computer says your colleagues from Portland P.D. want to know when she's out of the O.R. I'm sure you can let them know that. She's been assigned room 6D11."

"Can I go up and wait?"

"Under normal circumstances, no. But since you're a cop, I don't see the harm. 6D11—sixth floor then turn right and straight ahead through the doors. Just don't forget to call your office, or I'll hear about it."

• • •

Jim had been waiting ten minutes when an orderly wheeled in Sophie. She was groggy but recognized him. "Hello, Mr. Mountie. What are you doing here?"

"Came to make sure you were okay."

Two nurses followed the orderly and reconnected Sophie's systems. "The nurse could have told you that."

"I know. But since we just shared a decidedly intimate moment, I wanted to make sure myself."

"As you can see, I'm good. According to the doc, if the bullet had hit a couple of inches left, it could have been nasty. As it was, it missed everything important. So you were right—it's not serious. Being a cop I guess you've seen enough bullet wounds to judge what's what?"

"I've seen a few. Do you mind if I hang out until Portland P.D. gets here? They're going to need a statement."

Sophie gestured for Jim to sit.

"Sorry I ruined your hat."

Sophie smiled. "Applying pressure to a bleeding maw does play havoc with the gold braid."

"I hope it didn't hurt, me lying on top of you like that."

"No hurt. But a gentleman would have bought me dinner first."

"I really like your sense of humor," said Jim. "I image you're a riot when you're not all shot up and busted."

"Yeah, that's me, a regular Jay Leno."

"I'm told you fly for Granola Aviation."

Sophie nodded.

"Are they based here in Portland?"

"No, Phoenix."

"I just finished a case there."

"Aren't you a Mountie?"

"I was on loan to the Phoenix police department. Is Portland a normal route for you?"

"Granola Aviation is a charter company. We don't have normal routes like other airlines. I'm on assignment to Albatross Marine out of Lake Bluff, Illinois. They're moving corporate headquarters, and I'm flying in men, machines, and equipment for their new home somewhere up the Maine coast—Jonesboro, I think."

The hairs on the back of Jim's neck bristled the minute Sophie said "albatross." His beat ran from Ottawa to the ends of the earth, and he was following a narcotics trail that began in Pakistan, ran through Canada into Maine, and ended in New York. He'd followed the trail for some months, and, with an informant's hints and dogged detective work, had established that a group of disgruntled unlicensed fishermen was involved. A group locally known as the *Albatross Alliance*. Now, in more ways than one, Captain Sophie Berg was of interest to him.

"Wouldn't it be cheaper to do all that by truck?" asked Jim.

"I don't ask the reason why. I just do my job and pick up a nice, fat paycheck."

"Not exactly glamorous for the 'private pilot to the stars.'"

Sophie blushed. "Seems you've been reading the tabloids."

"I did get a glimpse of something that mentioned you and the rich and famous."

"And a total pain in the butt they all are," said Sophie. "It's like being nursemaid to a bunch of naughty kids who won't stay in their strollers. I lock myself in the cockpit until they disembark."

"What about all the pictures of you smiling and handshaking?"

"Ever heard of marketing?"

"Well, yes, I suppose there is that."

"And I'm guessing you've heard the rumors about drug kingpins and all?"

Jim swiped a finger across his lips. "Sort of."

"Is that why you're here?"

"No, though Portland P.D. might address that. I wanted to make sure you were all right."

Sophie shifted her position on the bed. "Well, I am. And, you know, don't believe everything you read in the newspapers. Some of us work damn hard and are proud of what we do. Ferrying around anybody in the drug trade isn't it. Now it's your turn. What's a Mountie doing in Portland?"

"I'm on assignment too, though I can't exactly tell you what I'm doing."

"A tall, dark, and handsome man of mystery. I think I like that."

An unexpected buzz ran through Jim's gut. He'd been attracted to the gorgeous pilot from the minute he saw her. Could she possibly feel the same? There was only one way to find out. "Good," said Jim. "So once they kick you out of here, is there a chance I can actually buy you that dinner you mentioned?"

Sophie grinned. "That might be nice. I'll be here a couple of days under observation, but should be back at the Regent by Friday."

Jim smiled satisfactorily. "You always stay at the Regent?" he asked.

"The company has a permanent rental there, so I guess that would be a yes. Where are you staying?"

"At a friend's log house up near Kezar Falls."

"Sounds like paradise. So what's a country boy doing in the big city?"

"Heading to the Regent for coffee."

"Coffee at the Regent? Sounds like an odd sort of place to have coffee. Ever heard of Starbucks?"

"The Regent uses a special Columbian blend I really like," said Jim, telling a little white lie. He'd been informed that a fisherman called Merrill, suspected of being involved with the Albatross Alliance, was in the counter side booth of the coffee shop. However, Jim's informant was unable to provide a description, other than to say he was in his sixties and average looking. With no other notable qualities, no extraordinary attributes, and no distinguishing marks, Jim was intending to position himself and use his lip-reading skills to gather information. "I was swinging by to get my favorite fix when we were shot."

"What *was* that all about?" asked Sophie. "Who would want to kill you?"

Jim raised an eyebrow. "I was about to ask you the same thing."

CHAPTER TWO

When he got back to his Portland office, Jim accessed the article the nurse had shown him on Granola Aviation. His curiosity piqued, he researched the airline and where it had recently flown. He was surprised to learn that in the previous year, Sophie and her colleagues had logged millions of miles crisscrossing North and South America and the islands. And now the "celebrity pilot" was in Maine, transporting men and machinery for Albatross Marine. Maine State Trooper Aaron "Mac" McKellin was assigned to partner Jim, and the young officer beamed as he approached his colleague. "Oh my, my. Once again, Mountie Jim gets his man, or should I say *woman*? Hear you and a lady pilot had a bumpy landing this morning."

"Very funny, Mac. Did your gal at Woody's Mercantile note any unusual purchases?" Jim knew that Woody's was the go-to place for local farmers, contractors, hunters, and fishermen. From outward appearances, Woody and his mercantile were operating above board; yet it was known that for a price, he could procure most anything. Moreover, he didn't care where he got it.

"You hurt much?"

"Bullet gashed my arm is all."

"So you won't be flexing those famous biceps for a while."

"What would you know about biceps?" asked Jim.

"I work out three nights a week at the Belly Up—"

"With thirty-two ounces of Bar Harbor Ale." Jim laughed. "Damage or no, don't get your hopes up. I can still arm wrestle you to the ground. So what happened at Woody's—did your informant come through?"

"She just said a couple of guys had her special order two dozen lobster pots. You know Woody stocks most anything for huntin', shootin', and fishin', but we're pretty far from the coast, so there's not much call for pots. When I pressed her, she could barely look me in the eye. I think Miss Billy Jo Waylon is nervous about something."

"Did she know if the guys were locals?"

Mac pulled out his notebook. "Her exact words were, 'Two peculiar guys came in, sounded like out-of-towners, and ordered the pots.'"

Jim scowled. "What did she mean by 'peculiar'?"

"Considering half the cats out there in the boonies are peculiar, you got me. You get anything from your fancy ass lip reading shit?"

"According to my snitch, a guy named Merrill was there, front and center in the counter side booth. Supposedly, he has something to do with the Albatross Alliance. But I never got into the Regent. Bullets flew before I hit the steps."

"Umm, what a coincidence," said Mac.

"My thought exactly. Something about the whole deal is niggling at me. I'm not a big supporter of coincidence."

"Had its perks though," said Mac. "You and the lady flyer ended up rolling in the dirt. Thought it was supposed to be hay?"

"You gonna keep on with this?"

"Might, for a while. It's not often we mortals get to grapple with a celebrity."

"So you know who she is?" asked Jim.

"Sure, wife gets that *Us* magazine. Captain Sophie Berg of Granola Aviation is in it quite often, and of course, after the shooting, she was all over the news. Channel seven said something about a possible investigation of Granola. The name makes them sound like a wholesome outfit, which completely belies their reputation for flying around dubious passengers. Are we looking into them?"

"Depends on who was being shot at—her or me."

"You think she's involved in something we're working on?"

"Don't know that yet. But what I do know is that she's moving materials from a company in Lake Bluff, Illinois to Jonesboro."

"So?" asked Mac.

"The company is called Albatross Marine."

"Jeez Louise."

CHAPTER THREE

Looking around the restaurant, Jim counted twelve couples, and could almost feel the vibes of celebration. Sophie had said the Regent's restaurant, Mary-Lou's, was *the* place for special occasions. His special occasion was finally pinning her down for the dinner they talked about. It had been a week since he'd seen her pale and in shock on the Portland pavement. Now, she was radiant in a secluded corner booth talking to a waitress.

Sophie smiled as he approached.

"I see you got here early," said Jim.

"It's an airline thing. Besides, it's a haul walking down all those stairs. Didn't want to be all hot and sweaty when you got here."

Jim raised an eyebrow and grinned. "Good thinking. Punctuality is a thing with me, too. So, I'm talk, dark, and handsome with a bod to die for?"

Sophie colored. "How do you figure that?"

"That's what you just said to the waitress."

"What the … " Sophie lifted the cloth and looked under the table. "Do you have the place bugged?"

"Nope," said Jim. "I lip read. You're very sweet when you interact with people."

"Oh really. Remind me to always keep my back to you."

"So, how are you feeling?" asked Jim, settling into the booth. "Any after-effects of your brush with death?"

"Apparently not. Doc signed me out A-1. I'm back on duty tomorrow."

"Then we can't have a celebratory glass of wine."

"You can," said Sophie. "Next time you can ply me with liquor."

"There'll be a next time?"

"Don't quite know yet. Let's see how you do this evening."

Jim smiled. "Deal."

"I can't remember whether I said it before, but thank you for protecting me. By all accounts, you saved my life."

"And thank you for so graciously cushioning my fall."

Sophie giggled. "So now the mutual admiration society has said its piece, any idea who was shooting at us and why?"

"I have a theory."

"Care to share?"

"Can't at the moment," answered Jim.

"Is that how it's going to be? I answer your questions, but all I get from you is, 'I can't talk about it'?"

"Sorry. Nature of the beast."

Sophie pouted. "Okay, I can live with that, for now. But let's assume I was the target; could it be because of the people I fly all over the place?"

"Do you have reason to believe it might be?"

"I'm not sure. However, I am sure I've pissed off a few people over the years."

"How so?"

"I'm a slam-clicker," said Sophie.

"What the heck is that?"

"I told you most of my passengers are a total pain in the rear, so I avoid them. There's been more than one drunken sot who thinks because he's leased the aircraft, he gets to bag the pilot. Goes for the crew too. Most of them join in with the partying just to say they've been with so and so. I might work around entertainers, but all their touchy feely nonsense isn't my style. On the aircraft, nobody enters my office. And when I get to the hotel, I slam the door and click the lock—slam-clicker. You won't see me until the next flight."

"That's a pretty solitary existence."

"I'm a workaholic with a master plan for my future and early retirement in an idyllic spot; I can be sociable then. Right now, as long as I get to indulge my passion for flying, I don't mind," said Sophie.

"Your being such a loner makes it less likely someone would want to shoot you."

"You'd think. But Granola Aviation is also about marketing, towing the company line, and selling the brand. They expect the staff to do whatever to drum up more business. You've probably seen my face in magazines and stuff, and that's where I draw the line."

"Weren't the terms of your job fully laid out when you signed on?"

"I'm sure they were. Except I was more interested in reaching my goal of being a captain. Now I realize Granola only took me on because of the way I look. I'm good PR for them."

"That's not all bad. You said yourself, you get to fly and draw a fat paycheck."

"There is that. But sometimes I irritate people because I ask questions about whom and what I'm flying around."

"Excuse me?" said Jim. "You don't have manifests?"

"We do, Mr. Know-It-All. Ever hear of falsifying documents? I don't actually check every piece of freight or eyeball every passenger."

"And that bothers you?" asked Jim.

"Well, *duh*. Even more so since someone shot me."

Jim made a mental note to dig deeper into Granola Aviation's operations. "What if the bullets were meant for me?"

"Oh, then it's all kosher. I feel great, no problems. Lead me to the tarmac."

Jim winced. "Did you agree to meet me for dinner just so you could find out how far we've gotten with the shooting?"

Sophie looked down. "Not exactly."

"Good, because I'm ravenous, and frankly I'd rather talk about you—Sophie. Not the hotshot Captain Berg."

"Being shot at doesn't bother you?"

"It does. But I can't crumble every time a felon takes aim at me."

Sophie looked surprised.

"Don't worry. It isn't as dire as it sounds. Now, I'm having a glass of wine, and halibut—what's your pleasure?"

"Club soda and the biggest piece of meat they have without a bone."

"I like a woman with an appetite," said Jim.

Sophie blushed, and Jim realized how she might have misinterpreted his meaning.

"Well that certainly didn't come out right," he said. "What I meant was I come from a family of restaurateurs, so it's genetic—I like people to eat."

"You like people to eat?" Sophie wasn't letting him off the hook.

"Oh, come on, you're killing me here. I don't like people to eat, nor do I like to eat people."

Sophie laughed. "Yeah, yeah, I get it, enough squirming. I've been to Ottawa many times—does your family have a restaurant there?"

"They're on number five, if memory serves. They own the Jacob Marley chain."

"I'm impressed; they're really good. How come you didn't go into the food biz?"

"I love to eat, but that's the sum total of my interest. I wanted adventure, excitement, and danger. Couldn't see getting much of that wearing an apron, so I joined the RCMP."

"Well we certainly have the hankering for adventure and excitement in common. But I'll pass on the danger. Artery clogging, biggest piece of meat without a bone is about as dangerous as my life gets."

Jim grinned. "You fly a metal tube forty thousand feet above the ground."

"Actually, thirty-seven is my max. Besides, it's the safest way to travel."

"That's what they say. How long have you been flying?"

"Since I was fourteen."

Jim raised an eyebrow.

"Private pilot's license, of course. My folks thought my being a commercial pilot was a waste of time. Despite what people might think, junior pilots get paid very little. The money only starts rolling in when you're a captain. So I actually got my first degree in psychology."

"That's impressive," said Jim. "But the flying won out?"

"Exactly. After I finished the psych degree, I realized I hated working in the field. It was so depressing and confining. But it was what my parents wanted, so I went along with it. After they were killed in an automobile accident, I realized how fleeting life is. I'd been flying the whole way through college, so I said, "I'm going to do what I'm passionate about, dammit."

"Sorry about your parents."

"I'm pushing thirty-five, so it was nearly ten years ago," said Sophie quietly. "And it allowed me to be me."

"Are you always so focused?"

Sophie smiled. "Curse of an only child."

"But you didn't start off in Granola?"

"No, I joined a regional airline in California and logged my hours. Then when I was offered the job with Granola, I practically ripped off the recruiter's arm. They were offering me 'captain' much earlier than any other airline would. The rest is history. What about you?"

"As I said—family of restaurateurs, but not my bag. I was fascinated by fifties cop shows, and being Canadian, I gravitated towards the 'glamour' of the Royal Canadian Mounted Police. I had these romantic notions about chasing the bad guys and getting the girl."

"You're not serious," said Sophie giggling.

"I was twelve; cut me some slack."

"So how's it working for you?"

"Good—I chase and catch bad guys." Jim grinned. "I'm still working on getting the girl."

• • •

Dinner passed pleasantly, and when Sophie suggested they take dessert and coffee in the hotel's lounge, Jim followed.

"I'm really looking forward to *Mary-Lou's Downfall*," said Sophie, handing him the desert menu.

"And that would be?"

"Ganache covered triple-layer chocolate cake, stuffed with fresh raspberries, and topped with whipped cream."

"Yikes, talk about living dangerously. Is that sharable?"

"Not on your life, buster. Get your own cake."

• • •

As the evening progressed, Sophie learned Jim was amusing and irreverent, and a self-confessed adrenaline junkie. He made her wince at his antics during police pursuits and kept her amused with his misadventures while potholing, white-water rafting, and sky-diving. And, like her singular passion for flying, it seemed everything he did, on or off duty, was about keeping him in shape to chase and catch criminals. Being a roving police officer was clearly a religion to him, and she really liked him for that. Moreover, she wasn't surprised to learn they had many things in common. At one time or another, they had each owned a British Racing Green Spitfire, imported from the U.K. Both had traveled extensively around Europe, had been horrified by the pretentiousness of Paris, refused entry into China—in Jim's case twice—and in one of life's bizarre coincidences, had been bitten by a rattlesnake.

As Sophie listened to Jim, memories of the men in her past flooded back. Jim had the same Mediterranean darkness, the same haunted, hazel eyes, and the same cavalier attitude about life as the others did. Good-looking adrenaline junkies seemed to be her norm—jerks who, in the end, cared more about their own satisfaction than hers; morons who simply wanted to flaunt her like one of their prize trophies. He was probably like all the rest.

Then she paused. Why was she judging Jim so harshly at this stage? He'd done nothing to get himself tarred and feathered. Quite the opposite. He'd been charming and attentive with charisma to spare; otherwise, he wouldn't be with her right now. She smiled. Might he be different from the others? And more importantly, did she even want to go there again?

"Penny for your thoughts," said Jim, touching her hand.

"Oh, sorry, I was miles away. Do you get lonely being constantly on the move to God knows where?"

"I've become accustomed to it."

"Do you ever miss having someone to come home to?"

"Sometimes, but it's a choice I made," said Jim. "Besides, it allows me to meet people like you."

"But I'll be out of your life tomorrow."

"No you won't."

Sophie laughed. "How do you work that out?"

"Once you've met me, you can never escape. I'm a Mountie, remember?"

"Right, you always get your man, but in case you hadn't noticed, I'm not a man."

Jim raised an eyebrow. "I'm making an exception for you."

"Is that a good thing?"

He reached across and traced tiny circles on her hand. "You tell me."

Sophie removed her hand. "You're pretty confident."

"When I find something I like, I go after it."

"And exactly what sort of a something in me do you like?"

Jim's gold-flecked hazel eyes focused on hers, leaving Sophie in absolutely no doubt of what was on his mind.

"Well, Sergeant Cromwell, I don't know about you, but I think we should finish up here before you set the drapes on fire."

"That obvious, eh?"

"Bingo."

Jim frowned. "It seems I may be overstepping my welcome?"

"Not exactly," said Sophie. "But I am flying tomorrow, and I need to get to bed."

"May I walk you to your room?"

"As long as you understand it's *my* room."

Jim stood and saluted comically. "Message received and understood, *mon capitan*."

•••

When they arrived at Sophie's room, Jim lingered at the door. "I'm a pretty spontaneous sort of guy," he said. "And I already warned you if I like something, I go right out and get it. Would you mind if I was really forward?"

"Depends—you're not going to slap the cuffs on me or anything, are you?"

Jim smiled and moved very close to her. "Fascinating as the prospect sounds, I was hoping we could start with something less drastic."

Sophie tingled as he kissed her. It had been an eternity since a man had kissed her in any way other than as a friend, and though her head told her to be wary, she kissed him back.

"I can do better if you let me," he whispered.

Sophie hadn't realized how much she'd missed the feel of a man's arms around her or the satisfying touch of his lips on hers. Still the nagging, sensible place in the back of her mind made her hold back.

Jim must have felt her reticence. "Am I moving too fast?" he asked.

"I'm a pilot," said Sophie. "You'll never be as fast as me."

"Then maybe we should go inside and test the theory."

"*Fascinating as the prospect sounds*," she mimicked, "I was hoping we could start with something less drastic."

"Sophie … " Jim pushed back. "Now you're just teasing me."

"No, Officer, Mr. Mountie, sir, I wouldn't dream of leading you on." Sophie kissed Jim passionately, and when he responded hungrily, it sent shivers through her body. However, the screaming voice of reason now accompanied her emotional alarm bells. She liked Jim, but her track record with men wasn't good. Best she remained concentrated on her career and thought about a relationship later. But it would be difficult. Jim Cromwell felt good, different, and somehow right. As welling desire accompanied the frissons running through her body, Sophie absolutely knew he was a lot more than she could currently handle. She pushed away. "Now that's teasing … "

Jim's voice was husky with anticipation and desire. "It's also not fair."

"All's fair in love and war."

"And which is this?" whispered Jim.

"Neither. It's preliminary negotiations."

Jim smiled. "I can negotiate real good."

"I'm sure you can. However, I have to fly to Miami and back tomorrow—"

"Miami? Thought your beat was Illinois?"

"I go where I'm told."

"So I'm telling you to go inside, and I'll follow."

Sophie pushed him away. "Not by you. God, if nothing else, you're persistent. Look, truth is, I'll be on a back-to-back rotation until the twenty-fifth, and right now, I'm not in the market for a one night stand."

Jim smiled. "Right now? So there's a possibility?"

"Hope springs eternal."

"Alexander Pope, 1688–1744."

"There's another thing I learned—you like poetry," said Sophie. "You're quite a character, and I'd like to know you better. Will you call me?"

"Promise."

Sophie backed into her room. "Good night for now." She had barely settled in when the phone rang.

"A promise is a promise," said Jim. "What are you doing?"

"I'm about to take a shower. How far did you get?"

"The lobby."

"Fool. Go home. I can't hang around talking to you. I'm standing naked on freezing tiles."

Jim laughed. "I could warm you up."

"I know, but I'll stick to a vigorous rub down from *Mr. Loofah*."

"No fair, lady, naked and wet, vigorous rub down—"

"Think of me in an avocado facial mask, ratty hair, flannel P.J.s, and bed socks."

"That did it!" said Jim, laughing.

CHAPTER FOUR

As Jim pulled up to the cabin's garage, the auto-light popped on. Moths circled the nightlight and made Jim smile. He loved to watch the huge, pale green *Lunas* as they rose and fell, and wondered why such magnificent insects only flew at night. He walked up the cabin's rise, savoring the peace and tranquility of his temporary home. In his line of work, it was a fleeting emotion.

As Jim entered the cabin's kitchen and flipped on the light—the maps and records he'd requested from various government departments taunted him from their place on the counter. He moved them to the dining room and hovered over a marine map covering the dining room table. However, his mind was full of thoughts he'd previously considered impossible during an investigation. They were of Sophie, and he needed to put his feelings for her in a compartment before he became totally distracted.

After pouring a shot of brandy, Jim set about cross-referencing the marine records with a Department of Fish and Wildlife printout. Highlighting all lobster-fishing centers from the Canadian border to Boston, he used a second list to hypothesize where a fisherman, already on the wrong side of the law, might mount an illegal hauling operation. He circled a dozen names and locations of men with rescinded or censured licenses. With the belief that one of them purchased lobster pots from an inland mercantile, he had a solid idea how drugs were getting across the Canadian border. However, proving it was problematic. The trail he'd been following didn't go to the ocean, but stalled in the depths of the local forest.

His informant had told him a local survivalist called Rake ran a methamphetamine lab out of an abandoned logging camp in the backwoods. Even though he didn't deal cocaine, Jim had no doubt he would know about drugs moving through his area. Thus, using another chart illustrating York County's intricate grid of logging trails and firebreaks, often used for activities having nothing to do with trees, Jim highlighted the suspected camps. A cursory look at the maps showed him why local law enforcement rarely located a methamphetamine operation. Not only did deep backwoods surround the camps, but many had severely compromised or no vehicle access. Moreover, with centuries-old canopies covering the target areas, helicopter crews had a hard time pinpointing sites. To proceed any further, Jim knew it was imperative he find the survivalist, Rake.

Feeling his investigation was about to get a lot more frustrating, Jim finished his brandy. As he sank back into his recliner, thoughts of Sophie again bit at his psyche. He'd become used to his monastic existence and couldn't see working any other way. However, when he came across someone like her, he couldn't help thinking what he might be missing. For some inexplicable reason, he couldn't get her out of his mind. Maybe it was because she was not only attractive, but also confident and witty—traits he particularly favored. Or maybe the notion of her working for a potentially shady outfit like Granola Aviation was the something he wasn't comfortable with, and it made him feel protective of her.

Within seconds of that realization, he fell asleep.

CHAPTER FIVE

When Jim arrived at his office the next morning, he was tired. Swirling images of lobster pots, an aircraft that became an albatross, and Sophie's face had dogged his sleep. Try as he might, he couldn't separate them. His state was not lost on his partner.

"Yo boss," Mac said. "Who's had you up all night? You look like shit."

"Just stuff," answered Jim. "There are coincidences popping up in the investigation, and they always bug the bejeezus out of me."

"Thought you might have had a busy night with the lady pilot."

"Well you thought wrong. For now, she's a possible connection. My interest in Captain Berg is strictly business."

"Yeah right, okay, boss, I'll buy that." Mac smiled. "Where do you want me today?"

"I think we'll both go back to Woody's. That lobster pot thing is niggling at me. When we were last there, I noticed a lean-to out back. Any idea what's in it?"

"Far as I know, carcasses. Woody hangs 'em back there for skinning and such."

"Looks a bit ramshackle to bear the weight, and the roof didn't seem high enough to hang much of anything."

"Now you mention it, it is low and in bad shape. Maybe it's empty."

"Don't think so," said Jim. "The dirt back there is weed-free and well-worn."

"Guns and ammo?" suggested Mac. "His licenses are current."

"It's possible. Whatever it is, the back of my neck is telling me there's something iffy going on. Why haven't you ever pinned anything on this Woody guy?"

"We can't establish he's done anything illegal. We suspect he's involved in shady dealings with weapons, but basically, he's a good old boy who pushes the limits of his licenses right to the edge. In the end, it's the same old story—too few cops in too big a monitoring area."

"Can't you stake out the place?" asked Jim.

"Been there, done that. But he has a network of watchers constantly updating him on our whereabouts."

"So who exactly is this guy?"

"Woodrow Thaddeus Rumford. His family has owned logging and mining companies for generations and has licenses to deal in explosives, munitions, basically anything that goes bang. He has connections in places you wouldn't believe, and if you ask me, I think that's the truth of why he keeps coming up smelling like a rose."

"Well I smell something, and it has nothing to do with roses or the assorted animal flesh he sells."

"So how big's that watch list of yours now?"

"Woody's, Jerry's Auto Body, the Well Head, and Mack the Knife's, locally, plus the Hole in the Wall, dockside, and Premier Freight at Portland Jetport. Then of course, there's Kickin' It Custom in New York."

"We're off the hook for New York," said Mac. "NYPD has a man in place. But right off, we have a problem with the rest. There are just four of us covering the boonies, and those businesses are spread all over the county. I'd ditch heavy-duty surveillance on Jerry's and Mack the Knife for now. You have to pass them every time you go into town, so they're easy to watch."

"Then we have to put the others through the ringer, one at a time," said Jim.

"By which time the bad guys have moved on."

"I can see the problem. Let me think about that a while. According to the local barfly, the go-to guy for all things meth is named Rake. You know anything about him?"

"Dang, is he on your list, too?"

Jim nodded.

"Well good luck with him. We absolutely can't pin that sucker down. He not only makes and deals; he's one of those survivalist nuts. You could be a foot away from him in the woods and not see him."

Jim ran a hand through his hair. "Gotta find him, Mac—he could be the key to everything. In the meantime, you stay local; keep your eyes and ears open for anything that might help. I'm going to find my snitch. I can't believe he doesn't know what this Merrill character looks like, and believe me, if that shit-head set me up, he's in a world of hurt."

CHAPTER SIX

Work had kept both Jim and Sophie on the move, so it had been ten days since they'd had dinner. "It's your favorite Mountie," he said into the phone. "How are you?"

Sophie laughed. "You have the most alarming timing."

"Come again?"

"This is the second time you've caught me stepping into the shower."

"Don't tell me; I'm about to get the brush-off amid a slurry of avocado dip and the vision of a flannel nightie?"

"It wasn't a dip, it was a mask, and it was P.J.s, not a nightie. For a cop you don't remember details too well."

"I remember details just fine," Jim whispered. "Like I remember you smell of Chanel Number 5 and your hair curls around your ears like tendrils on a vine. You have a little place on your neck that quivers when you laugh, and you have eyes blue enough to drown in. Need I say more?"

"Umm, I think you just about turned me to jelly," said Sophie. "Consider yourself exonerated. However, fair words notwithstanding, I can't hang around naked half the night—why didn't you call me sooner?"

"Work makes me single-minded. I just got back from chasing a lead on our shooting halfway across the state."

"Did you get your man?"

"No, but I will. Tomorrow is another day. Besides, I said I'd call today at the latest."

"Well thank you," said Sophie. "It's nice to know you're a man of your word."

"So how was Miami?"

"Didn't go. Froze my ass off in Lansing, schlepped to Knoxville, then back to Washington and here."

"All for Albatross Marine?"

"Don't really know—my paperwork said Golden Lance Historical Society. Once ops assigns us, our contracts are supposed to be binding. We don't usually do side jobs," said Sophie. "You're showing a keen interest in my roster—what gives?"

Golden Lance Historical. Jim's heart skipped a beat as the name echoed in his mind. Portland P.D. had reviewed security camera footage and had identified a Dodge Ram leaving the scene of the Regent shooting. It was registered to a Lance Deveraux. However, when Jim had gone to the address indicated on the DMV record, it turned out to be an empty lot. Jim had never liked coincidences, and with so many occurring around Sophie, he wasn't sure what to think.

"Just being a cop," said Jim, "busting with natural curiosity. Did you get passengers with the freight like Albatross?"

"Only one, which is just as well because all the freight was in the cabin."

"What sort of freight needs to go in the cabin?"

"Valuables, musical instruments, any number of things. Ops said my passenger was some sort of curator taking bales of valuable silks and tapestries to exhibitions."

"I get exhibitions in Washington," said Jim. "But Lansing and Knoxville? Not exactly the cultural capitals of the US."

"Now that you say it, it does seem out of whack. It would be exorbitantly expensive to charter an aircraft to schlep fabrics there."

"Is it a big deal when ops change your destination at the last minute?"

"Flying-wise, not really. I arrive at the airport, crank up the old gal's computers, and go. I have to tell you, though, the swapping and changing is getting irritating. And when I ask what gives, I get fobbed off."

"How?"

"Operational necessity, runway tolerances, impending weather—any number of half-assed excuses."

"But you're still getting that big fat paycheck," said Jim.

"True, though not much good if I get pneumonia and die before I can enjoy it. Besides, I was looking forward to enjoying a couple of days on Miami Beach."

"I'd enjoy you on the beach, too."

Sophie laughed. "I'm sure you would. So are we going to chit-chat about work, or is there a more personal reason for your call?"

"I'm assuming now that you're back, you get a couple of days off?"

"I do."

"Would you like to have lunch?"

"And?"

"You automatically assume there's an *and?*" asked Jim.

"I'm a gal, you're a guy; do the math. Where do you want to meet?"

"Nowhere. I'll pick you up at the hotel tomorrow. Eleven-thirty A.M., sharp."

"Eleven-thirty?" said Sophie. "That's not lunch for a charter flyer; that's the middle of the night."

"Then we'll explore the stars together."

"You are such a ham. I'll be in the lobby."

• • •

Jim couldn't miss Sophie. It wasn't just that she was a tall, striking blonde. She radiated an intangible something that set his senses reeling. And though he knew he was in danger of mixing business with pleasure, something he swore he'd never do, he couldn't help himself. He walked up to her and kissed her on both cheeks. "You look amazing."

"Thank you, kind sir. So where are we going for lunch?"

Jim smiled. "Naples."

"And you have a 747 parked where?"

"This Naples is on Sebago Lake. We're going to the Captain's Table. They serve the finest stuffed lobster in Maine—you do like lobster?"

"Let me at it. For an Arizona gal, a fresh caught lobster is nectar. Keep spoiling me and I may never go home."

"Maybe that's what I had in mind."

"Are you always so singular in your pursuit?" Sophie paused. "*Duh* … of course you are, you're a Mountie."

Jim flipped a salute. "I could have taken you somewhere more exotic—Egypt, Peru, Mexico, even China—but I figured we'd leave the long journeys for another day."

"All those places are in Maine?"

"Along with a bunch of others," said Jim. "I'd be happy to show you every one."

"How many are there?"

"A couple dozen."

"That's gonna take a while."

Jim flashed her a smile. "Precisely."

CHAPTER SEVEN

As Sophie was winging her way back to Phoenix and all points south, Jim was making the long haul up Route One North, to Gouldsboro, Maine, and a bar where petty felons hung out. Within the hour, an unshaven Jim, in grubby jeans and a t-shirt, pulled up outside a seedy rooming house over the Anchorman Bar in Gouldsboro. After depositing his bag in a dingy room overlooking the railroad tracks, he settled into a corner of the bar with a Molson and a burger. Always amazed at how talkative so-called professional criminals were with a few beers inside them, Jim listened intently to the scuttlebutt.

As the night wore on, Jim refilled his beer, but he was working on a tenth of the volume the locals were swilling down. Nevertheless, as eleven-thirty came, he was ready to wash off the tobacco stink and make notes on what he'd heard. However, as he took his last mouthful of beer, he heard a name that sparked his interest. He followed the voice to the end of the bar where a seedy-looking older man had asked for Lance.

A young blond, clearly gay and very intoxicated, swayed towards the man. "Daddy," he gushed. "You came for me."

"Come on, boy-o," said the older man. "Let's go. You ain't fixin' no boat if Daddy don't get you sober."

Waiting for the pair to leave, Jim approached the bar and ordered another beer. "Hey, chief," he said to the barman. "I got some problems with my boat. Was that Thompson, the boat builder?"

"Nah," answered the barman. "Old guy is Dante Goldwater, got a rust bucket in dock up the coast a ways. Young 'un is Lance Deveraux. He's a boat mechanic—damn good 'un when he's sober. Don't think I know any Thompson."

"A buddy told me to look out for him here; maybe I got the name wrong. Lance talk about working on anything right now? 'Cos my old baby needs some serious TLC."

"Dunno, go ask 'im. Goldwater drives a beat up Toyota truck."

Jim went to the door in time to see the truck leaving the lot. "Dang," he said to the barman. "Missed him. Might as well finish my beer; you know where they hang out?"

"Up the coast. Jonesport, I think—Blake Custom. Though I could be wrong. Heard tell it got bought out by some outfit from Illinois."

"Albatross Marine?" asked Jim.

"Yeah, that's it, Albatross. Knew it was some dumbass bird name."

Jim frowned. Golden Lance Historical at Granola—Goldwater and Lance here? It seemed his investigation was making a circle. And since he now knew that Sophie had been making waves at Granola, he wondered if she might have inadvertently asked a question that would reveal something they didn't want advertised. The notion that both he *and* she might have been the target of the bullets outside the Regent wouldn't leave him.

CHAPTER EIGHT

As he drove towards Jonesport, Jim began to understand what Mac had said about being a cop in a rural area. It took him over an hour at the sheriff's department in Machias to pick up the paperwork he requested. Fortunately, the documents had been worth the detour.

Using Merrill and Lance as the starting point, police computers had kicked out one Dante Goldwater Merrill who'd had several serious run-ins with the Coast Guard and police. His accumulated fishing violations had resulted in his losing his fishing license for life.

Another search, using Blake Custom Boat Mechanics as a starter, had revealed a Lance Deveraux had ordered specialized engine parts, customarily used to boost power on coast guard cutters. And while there was no police record on Lance, the hairs on the back of Jim's neck bristled as coincidences mounted. He picked up his phone.

"Yo, Jim, where you at?" asked Mac.

"On my way to Jonesport. You anywhere near Woody's?"

"Was there earlier, now I'm ten miles out."

"Can you swing back and talk to Billy Jo? Ask her what she meant by 'peculiar' about those two guys who ordered the pots."

"Way ahead of you, boss. They were gay."

"Why the hell didn't she say that in the beginning?"

Mac laughed. "Lot of heavy duty churchgoers in these parts. Gay is not a comfortable notion in their wheelhouse."

"By any chance was the pair an older guy, scruffy looking hobo type, with a good-looking young blond?"

"Hang on, let me pull over," said Mac. "Nope. She said the old guy was city dressed; that translates to expensive. Had an accent from away; that means not a local. And when she told him the damage, he paid from a huge wad of cash."

"Dammit," said Jim. "Doesn't sound like any hobo I know."

"The young dude was definitely blond though. In fact, Billy Jo said white hair. Oh, and he called the older guy, 'Daddy.'"

"Beautiful," said Jim. "That's close enough for me."

"What's shaking, boss?"

"Barman at the Anchorman gave me a heads up, and I think I'm finally onto our guys. I pulled a record for Dante Goldwater Merrill, and a Lance Deveraux turned up on an invoice for restricted engine parts going to Blake Custom. Stands to reason that anyone contemplating smuggling anything would need a boat that can outrun a coast guard cutter. And it would have to be inconspicuous. Ergo, tricked out fishing boat. I'm at the boatyard that ordered the parts, and I'm guessing someone not unfamiliar with local waters is thinking to upgrade their boat's engine."

"Hang on," said Mac. "Goldwater and Lance. Didn't you say your girlfriend shipped a bunch of stuff for a company called Golden Lance? Now that's a coincidence."

"Yeah, I already got that."

"Oh boy, Jim. You sure as hell can pick 'em."

"Okay, wise guy, still doesn't prove Sophie's involved in anything. She told me she's been making all sorts of waves when weird stuff occurs."

"Enough that someone would want to silence her?" asked Mac.

Jim took a deep breath. "I'd have to say, yes."

"Then we need to find the shooter and pronto."

"Ya think!" snapped Jim.

"Hey, Jim, I get it," said Mac. "I hope you're not getting too personally involved here."

"Sorry, Mac, tough few days. My gut is telling me all this is linked, but I can't believe Sophie is involved."

"How much does she know?"

"Not enough to convince her she might be in danger."

"Then I can see where you have a problem," said Mac.

"I can handle my end of things."

"Okay, you're the boss," said Mac. "You want me to follow up on anything?"

"Think it's time we looked at the airport. You know anybody?"

"Brother-in-law works at Beezer trucking."

"Good," said Jim. "Can you ask him what's been moving in and out? Whether anything suspicious has been happening?"

"Can do."

"And Mac?"

"Yeah, boss."

"Be discreet."

"Jim, please. I'm learning from the master."

• • •

When Jim parked at the boatyard, he saw the *Blake Custom* sign had been whitewashed over. And as he approached a ten-foot high chain-link fence that surrounded what appeared to be a deserted yard, two giant Rottweilers hurtled towards him. The dogs alone were incentive enough to keep anyone not wearing body armor on the roadside of the fence, so Jim got back in his truck and slowly cruised the perimeter. The panting monsters kept pace, and when Jim stopped again, he felt their eyes boring into him with undisguised menace. As he re-approached the fence, they didn't bark, but simply paced back and forth with tenacious resolve. Jim smiled. It was actually a sound tactic. Should a couple of huge dogs rush at you barking, you'd have a chance to turn tail and run. Approaching in silence would allow the dogs to be within striking distance before you knew what hit you. Clearly, the boatyard housed something somebody did not want advertised.

Reviewing his paperwork, Jim noted it had been over a week since the factory had shipped the restricted engine parts, so with luck, they should be waiting for pick-up in the building behind the dogs. And while he knew it was imperative he find out if the parts had been collected or not, as a good mechanic could install them in a couple of days, the Rottweilers had the advantage. He wasn't about to risk life and limb by coming up against two professional canines. Neither could he contact the boat builder for fear he'd alert Deveraux. So he drove to the far edge of the yard where a boat ramp ran down to the water.

Jumping from his truck, tape measure in hand, Jim began measuring the slip as if checking its acceptability to launch a boat. Then he continued beyond the fence line into the water. Jumping a small break onto a floating jetty, he continued measuring. Looking back, the boatyard showed no sign of life other than the two huge dogs slinking towards him.

Suddenly, the dogs hurled themselves into the water, barking furiously. However, they would venture no deeper than their heaving bellies.

Jim ignored their noise and continued slapping at pylons and pulling on mooring ropes. As he hoped, his position beyond the wharf's tidemark afforded him an unobstructed view of the boat-builder's launch bay. And there, tucked into a corner, partially hidden by a tarp, was a beat up Toyota truck with a large crate in the back. The bill of sale for the engine parts had indicated the size of the crate, and the one he was looking at fit the bill. But more telling, on each corner was the telltale purple anchor of the parts' manufacturer. He had his crate, and considering it would take a couple of days to install and test the parts, he knew approximately how long he had before things got really interesting.

After memorizing the Toyota's plate number, Jim jumped back to shore and returned to his vehicle. As he drove from the immediate area, he called in the plate number. He wasn't surprised to learn the vehicle belonged to Lance Deveraux, 1865 Longshore Drive, Crabtree Neck, Frenchman's Bay. If someone collected the crate that day and immediately installed the parts, it left Jim two days to set up a surveillance operation. Pulling out his map, Jim smiled; the bay's proximity to the Canadian border was not lost on him.

•••

It was late when Jim got back to his cabin. He was in month six, following leads from Ontario to New York. But it was the possibility that Sophie might be involved in the enterprise that consumed him. He knew telling her to get out while she could wasn't an option. If she was involved, she may warn her cohorts. If she wasn't, and his gut was telling him that, her sudden disappearance may alert the drug runners of his presence. His only choice was to deal with the current situation then head to Phoenix. There, he would take a closer look at Granola Aviation and see if Sophie could give him an inside take on the airline's workings.

CHAPTER NINE

Sophie picked up the phone on the second ring. "So, Sergeant Preston of the Yukon," she said playfully. "To what do I owe this pleasure?" Much to her surprise, Sophie had spent an inordinate amount of time thinking about Jim Cromwell. She had almost wanted him to be that jerky guy who floated in and out of her life. But every time she thought about Jim, it was with fondness and a growing need. Her past had made her nervous about commitment, and one part of her wanted to resist whatever it was he was showing her. However, she seemed to be losing the battle, and she didn't care. All she knew was, when he didn't call, she worried about him. When he did call, it made her day. And when she thought about what they might be, it made her smile.

"How did you know it was me?"

" *Duh*, caller ID. I'm a woman alone; I have to think about such things."

"You were obviously eager to hear from me."

"What makes you think that?"

"You picked up on the second ring. I'm a man alone; I know such things."

Sophie giggled. "I was merely passing the phone when it—"

"Yeah, yeah, tell it to the Marines. Do I guess you're on days off?"

"Sort of. I had another run in with my boss. I got suspended."

"Suspended? Christ, what did you do, crash an airplane?"

"No," said Sophie. "I caused a ruckus about carrying some freight, and got into a lost slot and mega delay situation, which cost Granola a hundred grand."

"Aren't captains allowed to question what freight they're carrying?"

"On a reputable airline. But it appears I'm working for Rinky Dink Air."

Jim laughed. "You suddenly came to that realization?"

"Not exactly."

Jim laughed. "So why did you refuse to carry the freight?"

"Actually, it was your fault."

"Me? What did I do?"

"You got me thinking, is what you did. Remember that shipment for Golden Lance Historical?"

"Sure, bales of fabrics and tapestries for exhibitions."

"And you said something about Lansing and Knoxville not being cultural capitals, exhibition centers, whatever."

"So?"

"The trip that got me suspended was a doozy, Miami to Medellín, Colombia, and the money was out of this world."

"So?"

"Stop saying 'so,' you monster. You started me on this personal revolution. I positioned empty to Medellín and was told I'd be returning via Kingston, Jamaica with coffee and more exhibition materials."

"Oh."

"Yeah. 'Oh.' First, have you any idea how much it costs to position an empty aircraft to South America? Then stopping off in Jamaica on the way back? Damn, Medellín and Kingston are definitely not the exhibition centers of the universe. And who the hell would take coffee to Jamaica, when they have some of the best in the world? My mind was full of your nonsense and it concluded there is only one commodity that would make the run cost effective. I'm thinking, 'Do these people take me for an idiot?'"

"That you are not," said Jim.

"Anyway, I'd barely had a minimum rest period, when ops called and said the shipper was ready to go. All the loading was done overnight and they wanted me to fly out at night. No big whoop there, but when I got to the aircraft and saw the same cockamamie bales of fabric in the cabin, it all hit the fan. I screamed bloody murder and called out customs."

"What did they find?" asked Jim.

"The night shift bozo, high on something other than life, turned up with a dog—"

"And found nothing untoward."

"Bingo. So I flew back as contracted, deciding to take it up with Kingston and Miami. Results were the same."

"So life in the fast lane is not all it's cracked up to be?" said Jim.

"Life in the fast lane is fine. It's the bozos in the other vehicles who need a kick in the derriere."

"You must have known when you joined Granola that being the only female captain would draw some flack? All that testosterone, thinking they can boss you about."

"If you're not going to take this seriously, I'm not talking to you."

Jim smiled. "Sorry."

"I don't mind being the token female; up to now it's worked for me. The money is fabulous and I get to be a captain."

"I assume you have the correct number of flying hours," said Jim.

"Yeah, I've paid my dues. But being in my thirties would have counted against me with one of the larger commercial airlines. It would have meant a few more years flogging away in the right hand seat."

"I can see where an ambitious, dynamic sort of gal would fight against that."

"There you go again, poking fun at me."

"Not a bit," said Jim. "Told you, I have a deep, abiding passion for a strong woman."

"Fool. You are so transparent."

"So now you're suspended."

"Actually, the chief pilot wanted me fired. However, the Director of PR and Marketing overrode him because I have publicity appearances. They compromised by taking me offline for two weeks."

"What happens now?" asked Jim.

"I didn't sign on to be a model or a non-flying spokesperson, which means I'm thinking about looking elsewhere for a job."

"Even if you aren't the captain?"

"I was blinded by all that nonsense. Jim, look, you know this isn't the first time I've made waves. Do you think I was shot at because I was asking too many questions?"

"First, I'm glad you're thinking of moving on. As for the shooting, I'm leaning towards a yes. The stuff I work on is shot worthy, and right now, I'm in the middle of something pretty intense. An intensity that keeps circling around to what's going on with you. Coincidences are occurring, the same names are popping up on both sides, and frankly, we really need to talk. I'm coming to Phoenix to put Granola on the spot. Would you have dinner with me?"

"Of course. Why don't you stay here?"

"At your house?"

"That's what 'stay here' usually means."

Jim hesitated. "That might prove to be a bit difficult."

"For whom?"

"Me, of course. I'm a guy, you're a gal; do the math?"

"Umm ... where have I heard that before?" said Sophie. "It's a four thousand square foot, four-bedroom house with a separate granny flat. I think that's sufficient room for me to hold you at bay."

"Four thousand square feet? My, my, Ms. Berg, they do pay you well."

"I told you."

"So, let's do this," said Jim. "I really have to do some intense investigation of Granola. Staying at a hotel would be less distracting for me. But I'd love to come to your house for lunch, and spend a few hours in your world."

"Spoken like a true gentleman. When can I expect you?"

"Is Wednesday good?"

"I'm not going anywhere. See you then."

• • •

As Jim pocketed his phone, a dozen scenarios ran through his mind, and all of them threatened to compromise his investigation. When they were shot, instinct had told him he was the target. Then the subsequent information he gleaned from Sophie led him to believe she was. Now, with a circular connection between Albatross Marine, the Albatross Alliance, Golden Lance Historical, Dante Goldwater Merrill, and Lance Deveraux, he realized they were *both* in someone's sights. And at the back of it all was Granola Aviation. Jim had no doubt they were using Sophie, but how was he to convince her of that? And more importantly, if she fell into something tangibly illegal, how was he to save her? Hopefully, going to Phoenix would help him find out something about Granola that might persuade her to get out. In the meantime, while his head told him any involvement with Sophie on a personal level was absolutely inappropriate, he found her hard to resist. Like a moth to a flame, he was drawn to her fire and knew that unless he could find who shot them, and break up the drug ring he was investigating before Sophie was pulled in too deep, they were both going to get burned.

CHAPTER TEN

Richard "Rake" Jensen was in his trailer in the woods. He fired up a joint and took a deep drag. Cele Jensen, his very pregnant, sixteen-year-old wife, rose from her battered recliner and yanked it from his hand.

"Ya get a job?" she slurred, sucking in the toxins like her life depended on it.

"Airport's dead, nuthin' in or out all day. Goin' back t'morra."

"So what the hell ya been doin' all afternoon?"

"Tryin' to get out from under you, ya grabbing bitch." Rake snatched back the joint.

"Y'ain't goin' no place without me," she snapped. "What I know'll get ya ten to twenty."

"Just get me another beer and keep yer trap shut."

Cele waddled past his chair. "Screw you, asshole."

"You wish … "

. . .

Portland airport was abuzz. Cops had raided the Premier Freight warehouse on the south side, discovering six dozen bales of marijuana packed in book crates, ready for trucking to Boston. The search and seizure resulted in a temporary closure of the facility. Across the road, the authorities cleared Beezer Trucking. However, by 7:00 A.M. , irate truckers, held up by the follow-up sweep, were snaking round the block waiting to offload their goods. With the warehouse situation progressing from minor inconvenience to seriously ugly, Beezer's dispatch pulled three guys from the pool of day laborers milling around the loading docks. Rake was one of those called, and an attending police officer asked for his airport clearance card as he stepped forward.

Considering how well he knew the dispatcher, Rake thought it unusual. Nevertheless, he handed over his dog-eared I.D.

"Last time you work here?" asked the cop.

"Coupla weeks maybe. Joe will know. I took my last order from him."

Joe nodded at the cop.

"Know any of those guys?" The cop asked Rake, gesturing toward a police wagon in which a dozen guys sat shackled.

Rake knew several of them, and at least two knew him as the local meth dealer. In fact, a week ago, he'd told them to "shove it" when they'd asked him to help move the shipment of marijuana for which they were now arrested.

"If they's worked here, musta seen 'em around," said Rake. "Other than that, don't know 'em."

Like most everyone he knew, Rake smoked a joint now and again. However, he never understood why anyone would risk being arrested for hauling weed. He knew from his own production and distribution chain there was a lot more money in crystal meth. For some time, he'd worked his lab in the woods around Victoria Falls, selling to weekenders and out-of-towners frequenting the bars of southern Maine. It was a sweet gig, but the drain of having a wife around made it a constant battle to get enough capital to expand his operation.

"So, day's a wastin'," said Rake. "Do I get the job or what?"

•••

Ten hours of backbreaking loading and unloading saw Rake back in the dispatch office. As he received his cash, Beezer asked him to work a full time fill-in. Full time meant an additional one hundred and fifty dollars a day under the table. That would not only make a dent in his chemical tab, but also give him a stash to ditch his wife and head up country. Rake readily accepted.

Dirty, sweating buckets, and in need of a beer, Rake left Portland airport and headed to the old port's Hole in the Wall. He'd arranged to meet Merrill, his chemical supplier. By profession, Merrill was a lobsterman from Frenchmen's Bay. However, Rake was one of the few people who knew he'd pled guilty to fishing violations in order to divert an in-depth investigation of his real job, the acquisition and transmission of narcotics. And Rake knew that knowledge was the only reason Merrill had extended him credit.

When Rake sauntered into the Hole in the Wall, a smoky beer-soaked dive on Commercial Avenue, he saw Merrill sitting in his corner nursing a stogie. The place was full of hard-working, honest stevedores and cargo chuckers, but anyone who needed a fix knew the man in the corner controlled the play. Rake slapped his c-note on the bar. "Usual," he mumbled.

"See Beezer's paying ya still," said the harpy pulling two large ones.

"Just shove one o' them over and quit yer yap."

After she made change, Rake left the coins.

"Allus was a big tipper," said the barmaid. "Dollar'll get yer happy hour whores durves." She smiled, her set of piano keys nursing a cheroot. "They's French, ya moron."

"They's just bowls o' trail mix an' beer nuts."

"Then take 'em, yer cheap bastard," she snapped.

Having eaten nothing all day, Rake balanced a bowl on each beer and turned to look for Merrill. The supplier's table was in the darkest corner by the kitchen door. Rake sidled along the bar and sat opposite the grizzled mariner.

"Y'ain't eatin' that," said Merrill, nodding at the bowls. "Shit's been out since Sat'dee."

"Don't care, I'm hungry, an' it's free."

"Na much good if ya crap for a week."

Rake continued munching.

"So waddaya want?" asked Merrill.

"Fixins."

Merrill grinned, teeth tobacco yellow. "Ya shittin' me, right?" he rasped. "Ya already two-fifty in the hole. Ya don't get nuthin' 'til I see some green."

Rake pulled money from his back pocket, peeled off sixty, and pushed it across the table.

"Wha the hell's that?"

"Alls I got right now," said Rake. "You'll have the rest next week; got a job lined up."

"So come back when ya got it all."

"Screw it, Merrill, gimme a break; you know I'm good for it."

"Ya was, ain't no more. Ya know the rule, no pay, no play; simple as that."

"Come on, old man, I gotta have stuff, I got customers—I owe 'em."

"Who'd be dumb enough to pay ya up front?"

Rake smiled. "Them as trust me."

"Ah, that's a good 'un. Hot damn, folks is plain stupid in some parts." Merrill took the cigar from his lips long enough to take a swig of beer. Before he returned his smoke to its resting place, he leaned conspiratorially toward Rake. "Ya get nuthin', 'less ya wanna help me out wi' sumthin'."

"Depends what it is," said Rake.

"Since when ya care what it is, long as ya get some green?"

"Turned over a new leaf."

"Bullshit," snapped Merrill. "Ya ain't got no more leaves to turn."

"It's what then?"

"Fishing expedition."

"Aw, come on, Merrill, you know that lobster crap gives me the trots."

"Ain't lobs. Me, you, an' one other is pickin' up specialty goods from Canadia an' movin' it to Boston. Pays fifty large apiece."

"Fifty apiece? What the freak we movin'?"

"Snow," whispered Merrill.

"Risk?"

"Some."

"For fifty large, must be more 'an 'some.' Been done before?" asked Rake.

"Nah—that's the beauty. First run; got nobody lookin' on."

"How's it getting in?"

"Ain't your bizniss."

"Then I ain't doin' it."

Merrill sucked hard to the end of his smoke and crushed his stogie into the empty trail-mix dish. "Sometime I dunno why I bother wi' yo' trailer trash."

Rake leaned forward. "'Cos I can haul ass and keep my mouth shut."

"Certain Paki shipper moves tons o' crap for his *brothers* in Toronto and Montreal. There's hundreds a boxes o' useless shit, but among the spices an' knick-knacks is snow. Friend o' mine in air cargo sorts da shipment before it gets ta customs, and routes the good stuff to Saint John. Don't know how—don't wanna know. All I's interested in, he puts the snow in my pots off o' Grand Manan. We take off from Frenchman's, haul 'em pots outta da water, run down to Zeb Cove t' waitin' trucks, and let out to Boston. Piece o' piss, and we get fifty apiece. You in?"

"When?"

"Day after t'morra—you in?"

"Gotta see about gettin' off work."

Merrill scowled. "Don't be a shithead; ditch it. Beezer ain't payin' no fifty large."

"Nah, gotta have an alibi. Cops is all over the warehouse 'cos of some shit going down next door."

"Call in sick; ain't like yer known fer reliability."

"Okay," said Rake, processing the plan. "I'm in. What time?"

"Come te Frenchman's t'morra. We head out first light Wensdee, you kin stay over." Merrill pulled a card from his pocket. "Here's directions. Ring da bell, you'll be let in."

"What about some supplies on account?" asked Rake.

"Ya got balls. Back o' my truck, left side."

• • •

The drive back to Victoria Falls was easier than it had been for some time. Rake knew exactly what he'd do with fifty grand, and it didn't involve the whiny fat bitch he was married to. Up in the northern townships, he might freeze his ass off, but he knew guys who knew guys running the militia. They'd pay plenty for weapons and a decent jug of whiskey, so he'd see Woody about a bunch of munitions, haul some supplies, and do some trading. Rake smiled as the thought crossed his mind. With the proceeds from the sales, he could disappear for a while and live pretty good with one of them nympho' militia chicks.

Bypassing his turn into the woods, Rake headed to Woody's on Route 160. He cautiously approached the mercantile and drove on by. Seeing no sign of activity, he doubled-back and pulled carefully under the lean-to at the back. The structure, barely high enough to fit a truck, was purposefully low to dissuade casual customers from parking there. However, special patrons knew it was doable, and it protected the store's rear door from passing scrutiny.

Rake opened his truck door and, avoiding the closely situated posts, stepped into the deeply shadowed lean-to. He had to duck to avoid rapping his head on the roof, and reaching up at the convergence of the ceiling and wood and steel frame, he flicked a switch. It released the back building's light outer door, exposing another, made of steel. It had a sophisticated locking mechanism.

Rake punched in his personal code, and the heavy door swung noiselessly open.

Before he'd been part of Woody's inner circle, Rake had always thought the entrance at the back unusual. However, one glance at the vault's contents revealed the need for the advanced security procedures. All manner of munitions were hung or stacked against the walls. Woody had licenses to sell weaponry and hunting equipment, as well as explosives for mining and construction outfits. That notwithstanding, it was well known to local entrepreneurs in the shadows of the law that for the right price, he could procure most any ordinance the army of a small country might wish to use.

When the steel door's lock-release activated a security camera, it alerted Woody, who stepped into the vault. "Hey bro', how's it hangin'?"

"Sweet," said Rake, bumping his friend's fist. "What's been happnin' here?"

"Had some state pig creeping around. Rumor has it he's tied up with a Mountie and thinks I'm gonna help 'em wi' some Canadian shit. Fat freakin' chance; they's all shitheads, useless as a tit on a bull. What can I do ya for?"

"Half rack of M-16s, couple of AK-47s, ammo belts, case of incendiaries, and a can of grenades."

"Hot damn," said Woody. "What ya startin', world war three?"

"Takin' me a little vacation up in the territories. Thought I'd make some trade wi' the brethren and start over."

"When you need 'em?"

"Couple of days."

"Gonna cost," said Woody.

"I got prospects."

"Need more'n prospects, bro'. Gonna cost some major grand."

"S'okay, I'm gettin' fifty."

"Sweet. What ya' movin', buddy—got a piece for me?"

"Not up to me, Wood, or I'd see ya right. Guy outa Frenchmen's is payin'."

"Old guy, smokes stogies, smells like a fish market three days after a heat wave?"

"Ya know 'im?"

"Sure, Merrill's a peach. He says you gettin' some green an' it's money in the bank. Creepy old shit's a legend up north, moved more merchandise than I've had cheeseburgers. Cops ain't able to touch 'im. But watch 'im, bro'. He got ice water in his veins. He'll drop ya like a buck on opening day if he thinks ya ain't cuttin' it."

"No sweat, I can handle him."

"Awright, long as you're prepared. Felt I had to give ya fair warning." Pulling a half pencil from behind his ear, Woody made a note of Rake's requirements. "Ooo-wee, this some sweet hardware, bro'. Once I got 'em, ey can only stay here twenty-four hours. This shit's way hot to screw around."

"I'll pick 'em up Friday."

"Up front?"

"Woody, I'm bummed. It's me—since when we don't trust each other?"

"Since you owe me crystal, bro'."

"Yeah, you're right; I'll fix that today, you got my word."

Woody nodded and the two bumped fists.

• • •

Within the hour, Rake was at his trailer hauling in supplies. And as he worked on his next batch of meth, he processed what Woody had said about Merrill. He wasn't entirely happy about payment *after* the shipment was delivered to Boston, for despite Woody's confident assertion that Merrill knew what he was doing, Rake didn't trust the old bastard.

When he climbed into bed, Rake woke his wife and gave her a healthy dose of what kept her sweet. It was deliberate. And he knew another five-minute roll in the morning would be enough to persuade her to drive him to work. It was all part of covering his ass.

CHAPTER ELEVEN

Sophie's hadn't remembered Jim being so handsome. He stood outside her front door, his hair shining like ebony in the midday sun, and when he removed the sunglasses, his expressive hazel eyes fixed on hers with an intensity she found disturbing. She tried blinking to prevent becoming lost in their darkness, but was inexorably drawn into their depths. Never having experienced that feeling before, she blushed. In the instant the realization hit, Sophie wasn't sure how wise it had been to invite such a man to her house. She couldn't deny that whatever he projected was exciting, and his blatant sensuality rejuvenated her. Now he was at her house, radiating enough testosterone to light up Phoenix, and she could no more turn him away than forget to breathe.

"Hi," said Jim. "Can I come in?" He stepped forward and kissed her on both cheeks. His face remained close to hers. "You look different, content, like the cat that got the cream. I like it."

"I am absolutely the same as the last time we met, so stop all the flattery and come inside. How did your time at Granola pan out?"

"It was frustrating. They were clean. Too clean. Bending over backwards to accommodate. I couldn't find anything untoward, and that in itself in such a big company is odd. Like you said—something just doesn't feel right."

Sophie smiled. "Now you know what I feel like every time I ask questions. So is this meeting business or will it be pleasure?"

"I imagine that's up to you," said Jim.

"No, it's not. I'm not stupid, Jim. You came out here to investigate Granola Aviation, and you didn't come to see me on a whim. First and foremost you're a cop. You might keep everything close to your chest, but I know you well enough to realize that at some point, you thought I had something to do with whatever is going on there."

Jim brushed a finger across his brow. "I have to admit, I did. However, events have clarified my thinking on the subject."

"And that leaves me where?"

As soon as the door closed, Jim reached for Sophie's hand, and tenderly brushed his lips across her fingertips. "I missed you."

"It's only been a few days."

"And nights. Did you miss me?"

She pulled back her hand. "I don't know you well enough to miss you."

Jim pouted comically. "I'm crushed. Dammit woman, I thought we had something special. We shared Lobster Thermidor and Mary Lou's Downfall." He theatrically placed the back of his hand to his brow. "If to her share some female errors fall, look on her face and you'll forget them all."

Sophie giggled. "Good grief, you really do like Alexander Pope. If chocolate cake gets you this fired up, I'd better nix the brownies with coffee." She gestured to a couch. "Sit."

He saluted smartly. "Yes, ma'am!"

Sophie liked his easy way with her, but now that he was in her home, his flirting seemed too intense. Setting up the coffee tray, she turned to ask him a question. He was right behind her. "Whoa—stealth mode. Do they teach you that at the RCMP academy?"

"Correct. They also teach us survival skills and interrogation techniques. So did you miss me even a little tiny bit?" He gestured with his thumb and forefinger.

"Granola rescinded my suspension, ergo, I've been too busy."

Jim's eyebrow rose. "They say why you're back on line?"

"Pilot rostering SNAFU, increased workload, special contract."

"Those things normal?"

"At Granola—what's normal?"

"So where have you been?"

"Milk run," said Sophie matter-of-factly. "Over-spill freight up and down the Eastern seaboard."

"And you didn't think to call me?"

"Max flying hours with minimum rest time doesn't make me very sociable."

"So what can I do to ease your burden?" He ran a finger lightly down her cheek.

"For a start, you can grab the shortbread and follow me."

Jim obediently followed, and sat on the sofa opposite her.

Sophie found it impossible to ignore the magnetism radiating from him, and as she poured coffee, she imagined his antics had swept countless women off their feet. Would she simply be one more? In her heart, she knew such an empty gesture would consume her, so she cast the thought to the recesses of her psyche. "I don't remember your gaze following me so intently. What's up?"

"Just making sure there are no aftereffects from your brush with death."

"And you can tell that by watching me pour coffee?"

"Checking out your ADLs."

"ADLs?"

"Activities of Daily Living. They're very important to assessing a patient's full recovery. Do you only know about pilot stuff?"

"Cheeky monkey, I know plenty of stuff." Sophie took several seconds to find her inner focus. "Jim, this is pretty awkward, but I have to ask. Is it possible I'm one of the bad guys, that I've helped them do something really wrong? Even if I didn't know it?"

"If you believe you're in amongst bad guys, why are you still working for Granola?"

Sophie frowned. "You're not supposed to answer my question with a question."

"It's valid."

"Okay. So, apart from being given the opportunity of a lifetime, and setting aside living my dream and the fantastic paycheck, I guess I'm still with them because I haven't seen any actual proof that Granola is doing anything untoward. The thing not feeling kosher doesn't count."

"Point taken. Why are you sitting way over there?" said Jim, patting the sofa cushion.

Sophie smiled. "It's safer."

"Safer. Don't you feel safe with me?"

"Something like that."

Jim got up and knelt beside her chair. Taking her hand, he placed it on his heart. "I'm a cop, you can trust me." Then he winked at her.

His levity broke the tension, and Sophie couldn't help laughing. Nevertheless, she pulled her hand away. "If, in one brain cell, you think I'm a bad guy, you should not be flirting with me."

"I know."

"So why are you doing it?"

"Because I can." Jim pulled her to her feet. "Seriously, Sophie, I don't know what happened between us, but I have this connection with you. From the moment we met, I felt it."

"Of course you felt it; you were sprawled on top of me."

"Correct. However, setting aside your inner cynic, I want you to know how very much I like you. And it's not simply a physical thing. It's something deeper. I can't explain it right now, but given time, I will."

When he tried to kiss her, she shrank back. "Jim, I know I said … well, I invited you here … but … er … I'm not sure I'm ready for someone like you."

"Someone like me?" asked Jim.

"I've dated guys like you. Jeezum, I always date guys like you. Guys who say and do exactly what they want in the moment.

It's confusing and overwhelming. But it comes down to me not wanting to be just another notch on your bedpost."

"You'll never know until you try."

"See, that's what I mean," said Sophie. "What if I'm not what you expect? Come over here." She led him to the hall mirror. "Look at you, you're drop dead gorgeous."

"I know."

"Immodest, but nevertheless charming. You're funny and intelligent. You know exactly who you are and what you want. Good grief, you quote Alexander Pope. You could have any woman you want. Why on earth would you want to be with a woman who would think more about her aircraft than you?"

"Is that what's bothering you?" asked Jim. "You choose to put your career ahead of a relationship."

"Most guys can't handle that."

"I'm not most guys. I like your independence. My lifestyle wouldn't suit a woman who needs to know where I am and what I'm doing every minute. We think alike, Sophie. You'll let me do my thing, and I'll let you do yours. You're exactly what I want."

He pulled her close and kissed her.

• • •

They spent the afternoon by the pool. Jim was wearing shorts but Sophie had changed into a purple bikini. He couldn't help admiring her athletic body with curves in all the right places, and wondered what it might be like to have her long legs wrapped around him. Though he wanted very badly to make that happen, he knew from his conversations with Sophie that romance was not on her immediate agenda. So he kept the conversation as formal as his libido allowed by talking about their jobs and the isolation of being a workaholic.

As the sun went down, Sophie touched Jim's arm. "I'm getting a glass of wine—you want one?"

"Nah. I'd rather not drink—even just one—and then drive on unfamiliar roads. Have you any idea how convoluted your highway system is? People come at you from ten sides at once, and *hello* turn signals?"

Sophie laughed. "You've been in the boonies way too long. Welcome to the metropolis."

"Unless the wine is an invitation."

"Invitation?"

Jim grinned. "To stay here."

"Not so fast, Casanova. I applaud your bold approach, and might even learn to appreciate the unbridled enthusiasm. But not today. I'll bring you a Perrier."

When she returned with the drinks, Sophie had put on pants and a blouse. "Got to warn you, it gets cool real fast when the sun goes down."

"I know. But I'm Canadian—good, thick blood. I'm gonna soak up all the sun I can get."

"You mentioned friends in Arizona," said Sophie. "Are you seeing them while you're here?"

"Don't think so. They live in Prescott Valley."

"That's only a couple of hours north."

"I know, but as you said, I came here to look into Granola." Jim gestured towards Sophie. "And … see you of course. Besides, I have to get straight back. My case is moving fast and I have a rendezvous with some fishermen."

"Umm, a workaholic who takes time out to go fishing."

"It's not that sort of fishing."

"Can you talk about it?" asked Sophie.

"Not at the moment. But enough of that. I only have a few hours; let's concentrate on you."

"Is that a good or bad thing?"

"Depends. Does it bother you that I spent the last two days pulling apart Granola Aviation?"

"Why should it?"

"Because my gut is telling me something is going on there and when I figure out what it is, things could get messy. Our relationship might prove awkward."

"Our relationship? We've had a couple of fairly innocent kisses."

"What if something else develops?"

Sophie smiled. "It only will if I let it."

"That put me firmly in my place."

Sophie reached for his hand. "Jim, there is no place right now. I'm a career woman, always will be. I'm game for drinks and good conversation now and again, but anything more is—"

"Not in your master plan?"

Sophie smiled. "Why, Mr. Mountie, I do declare you're hurt. I guess you aren't used to rejection."

"I get rejection aplenty—just not after someone invites me to her house."

"So let's get it straight. I already gave you my master-plan speech, so you know I'm focusing on my career. And I'll take rejection off the table because, strictly speaking, I'm not doing that."

Jim leered and grinned.

"Oh puleez," teased Sophie. "Let's say I'm simply honing my life's priorities."

"Ah-ha. The priorities clause. Is there wiggle room?" Jim pouted theatrically. "Is there any hope for me?"

Sophie smiled. "How about we take it a step at a time? We have the drinks, and now we converse."

"And what would you like to converse about?" asked Jim.

"Considering my tenuous position, I understand you can't talk about the specifics of what you're working on. And I'm assuming that since I haven't been arrested, and since you're here making overtures towards me, that I'm not on your suspect radar. However, you are first and foremost a cop, so you're probably itching to ask me some work related questions."

Jim laughed. "Very good, Captain Smarty Pants. Why were you nervous about hauling freight out of Columbia?"

"I told you on the phone, that was your fault. All your talk about bales of *fabric*," Sophie gave Jim the "quote" fingers. "Going to cities not known as exhibition venues. You made me nervous, so I hit the panic button, and called out customs."

"It can't just have been my ten cents worth. Something else must have sparked in the back of your mind."

"Why? It was you, plain and simple. My mind went into overdrive and suddenly I'm thinking about being caught hauling drugs and all manner of nonsense."

"I had no idea my words are that powerful."

"Be serious, Jim. This is my career we're talking about. I don't want to be associated with anything illegal. I also don't want to be known as micro-managing nudge who questions every facet of my aircraft's operation. I could lose everything I've worked for."

"So it bothers you."

"Of course it bothers me," said Sophie.

"Then hopefully you'll be open to helping me clarify a few things."

"Of course, fire away."

"Remember that trip you did for Golden Lance? Would you recognize your passenger again?"

"I saw him once, for two minutes tops," said Sophie.

"Describe him."

"Short, cultured, well-dressed."

Jim smiled. "That narrows it down to half the businessmen on the planet. Was there anything strange about him?"

"Not that I remember."

"Where were you parked when the goods were loaded?"

"Cargo ramp."

"With customs and the whole nine yards," asked Jim.

"I presume. I told you, we get the load-sheet and trust that cargo and loading have done their job. We don't check what we carry. Except at Medellín, of course, and we know how that turned out."

"Anyone else at the aircraft seeing off this dude and his fabrics?"

"VIP handing was there, dispatcher, load control, the usual crowd." Sophie paused for thought. "Oh, and the guy's son, I think."

"Son?"

"Well, he said, 'Goodbye, Daddy, see you in a few days.'"

The hairs on the back of Jim's neck bristled. "What did he look like?"

"A son."

"*Sophie* ... " said Jim impatiently.

"Good looking, slight, blond."

"How blond?"

"Excuse me."

"His hair," asked Jim. "How blond?"

"Almost white, like Lady Gaga in her platinum persona."

CHAPTER TWELVE

After four hours on the road, Rake coasted to a halt at the Jellison Cove boat launch parking lot, and ditched his rental. Most of the fishing boats were at sea, so he easily picked out Merrill's vessel. Aptly named the *Hesperus*, it didn't inspire confidence.

As directed, he walked across the parking lot towards the seafront bluff, where a row of large houses looked out over the ocean. Then taking the path below the houses down to the water, he found himself beside a dilapidated fishermen's shack. Rake checked his directions as a thought crossed his mind. Maybe Merrill wasn't as successful as Woody said because this place made Rake's trailer seem luxurious. A battered and deeply pitted ship's bell hung on the door. He tapped it, and a filthy window slid open, revealing a young man's face.

"Oh my, aren't you a sight," said a surprisingly cultured voice. "Do I have the pleasure of addressing Rake?" The disembodied head had finely chiseled features and dyed platinum blond hair.

"Yeah. Merrill around?"

"Out back—come in, my dear. Mind the steps and duck."

Rake didn't and smacked his head sharply on the door jam.

The young man giggled. "Oh my, lovely body, but clearly no brains. That," he pointed a manicured finger in Rake's direction, "is going to leave a mark." And when he moistened the finger and reached out to dab the place that had connected with the door jam, Rake stepped back sharply.

"Shit, man, what the fu—"

"You're going to have to be a lot more careful about following orders."

Rake had had no idea Merrill hung around gays, and his fists clenched. "Try that again and I'll punch your lights out."

"My, my, aren't we a touchy pussy."

Rake focused on the money and proceeded into the comparative darkness of the shack. As his eyes adjusted, he could see he was being led to an open closet.

Inside the door jam, the blond reached up and activated something, which popped a door at the back. "Go on through."

Rake stepped into a dimly lit fieldstone cellar with stairs leading up. "This crummy place has a cellar?" he asked.

"This crummy place has everything. Now, upsy-daisy," said platinum blond, pointing up the stairs. "Onward and upward, the door isn't locked."

Rake proceeded up the stairs, wondering what sort of shit he'd gotten himself into. He was more intimidated than he'd been for some time, and when he cautiously opened the door, he was surprised to be standing in a space decorated like the anteroom of an uptown lawyer's office.

"Go right on in, sweet cheeks," said platinum blond, menacingly close to Rake's ear. "Walk forward to Daddy."

Rake braced for trouble, and when an appreciative whistle accompanied the feel of a finger running down his tensed biceps, he lashed out.

"*Tsk, tsk, tsk*, such fruitless aggression," said platinum blond, dodging around Rake into the next room. "Follow me."

Rake followed into a large, expensively decorated room, and there, pawing over a chart on an antique table, was Merrill. Scrubbed pink and dressed in silk pajamas, had he not been sucking on his trademark stogie, Rake wouldn't have recognized him.

"Hey, Rake," said Merrill, exhibiting none of the broad coastal accent that was customary from him. "You made good time. Come take a look at this chart. You'll need to get a handle on the pick-up zone."

"Who's the blond?" asked Rake.

"Lance Deveraux, best engine man in Hancock County." Merrill smirked as he beckoned Lance forward. "Come give your daddy some sugar."

Lance stood his ground and blew Merrill a kiss.

"He's a pip, ain't he?" said Merrill. "Makes more than one of my engines purr like a top."

Rake frowned. "What the hell is—"

"Seems our Rakey has an itsy-bitsy hang-up, Daddy," said Lance.

Merrill smiled. "His loss. Now step lively, both of you, and take a look here."

Rake relaxed as much as his disgust would allow and approached the table.

"Okay. We have twenty-four pots in groups of six here, here, here, and here. They shouldn't be too much of a problem; they're close together. However, this is what you have to commit to memory." Merrill took a drag on his stogie. "We'll be hauling up, emptying, and putting the pots back, so we have no time for duplication. Memorize the pattern for each six. You got it?"

"Sure," said Rake. "Piece of cake. As long as you pull alongside this first bunch we can run around in figures of eight."

Lance poked Rake's shoulder. "Not so dumb as you look after all."

"Fuck you, asshole."

"*Oooo*, but such a nasty mouth."

"Quit it, you two," barked Merrill. "Scratch out each other's eyes after the job's done. We've got this down, Rake, but you need to know it with your eyes closed. Study it good and get an early night; we set out around four." Merrill could see the question in Rake's eyes, and reverted to his accent. "Sort o' surprisin', ain't it? Like all 'em losers, ya thought I's a filty bum, didn't ya?"

Rake smiled. "Least I know why the cops ha' never caught up with ya."

"Well don't let anybody's demeanor deceive you, least of all mine. No one is exactly who or what they seem, and because of that, we need to get one thing straight. I might trust you for now, but in the big scheme of things, it's all about me. I call the shots and you will do as you're told, or I'll drop you like the plague. You can go anywhere in the house but there." Merrill pointed to a door. "I have cameras running twenty-four-seven so don't think you can sneak in while I'm sleeping. There's grub and booze in the fridge; help yourself. But go easy on the sauce. I don't want you too pissed to haul up those pots fast. *Comprende?*"

"Yeah. What about the Boston end?"

"All you need to know is once we hit land, haul ass to the parking lot of the empty warehouse behind the Orient Heights train station. And don't get any ideas. The gentlemen who contracted me to deliver the merchandise don't like skimmers. Understand?"

Rake nodded sheepishly. He was still trying to digest that the man in front of him was entirely different from the Merrill he'd been doing business with for two years.

"Lance," continued Merrill, "did you keep the catch from today in case we get stopped?"

"I did—also some from yesterday and the day before."

"Good boy, now scoot off and load up. I want to be ready first light."

"Whatever you say, Daddy." He blew Merrill a kiss. Then wetting his index finger, wrote an air "one" in Rake's direction.

Merrill smiled in a way that turned Rake's stomach. "He's really something, ain't he?"

Rake snorted. "He's a fag."

With lightening reflexes belying his age, Merrill clamped vice-like fingers around Rake's throat. "Shut it, ass wipe. Ain't nobody's business but ours who we choose to share a bed with. You got a problem with that, split now, and die tomorrow. And make no mistake, if the shit hits the fan and I have to choose one of you, it ain't gonna be no Rake Jensen."

"Didn't mean nuthin' by it," croaked Rake. "Just didn't peg you for a—"

"Say it and I'll drop you right here. Shouldn't make no never mind what all I do, unless you got your own designs."

"Sorry, man, ease up, you're choking me."

Merrill shook Rake by his neck. "Don't you ever wonder why shits like you whore round from woman to woman? Who you trying to convince, cupcake?" Merrill ran his other gnarly knuckle down his captive's cheek.

Rake's jaw tightened, but he said nothing.

Merrill smiled and let Rake go. "You're a beautiful thing, but you ain't convincing me one little bit, Mr. Man."

When he heard a delicate cough behind him, Rake spun round.

Lance was smiling broadly, hands on hips. "Gets right to the heart of you, doesn't he?" He minced toward Merrill, and led the old man to their bedroom.

As the door closed, silence descended, but within minutes, the rhythmic sounds of lovemaking assaulted Rake's consciousness. With anger broiling from Merrill's insinuation, he picked up the remote. Flipping the channels, he found Playboy, and as the antics of several consenting adults filled the screen, he drowned out the real life lovers with an orgy of the cinematic kind. Then upon raiding the fridge, he poured the better part of a pitcher of Tom Collins down his throat.

• • •

When Lance kicked Rake from sleep, he'd been banging three women in a room full of snakes. He didn't mind Lance getting him up because he hated snakes, and one of the women even looked like his wife. When he heard cooking sounds coming from the kitchen, he stood and un-kinked himself from the position in which he'd collapsed in an armchair. "Holy crap," he mumbled, shuffling into the kitchen.

"We do have beds," said Lance, waving a spatula in the air. "Just because you convey this macho persona doesn't mean you have to behave like a bum."

"Screw you, fag."

Lance smiled. "Put the claws away, sweet cheeks; Daddy won't like them. Now tidy up, you look like shit. There's coffee, eggs, bacon, and hell, I even made you toast—how plebian. Eat quickly because the alert members of this team are ready to go."

Rick launched the finger at Lance before slapping bacon and egg between two slices of toast and setting off back through the closet.

CHAPTER THIRTEEN

Jim was on the look-out perch of the fishing boat *Nellie Bligh*, circling the lobster beds off Grand Manan Island. When he panned his binoculars over the ocean, he spotted a series of purple and gold buoys, similar to those sold by Woody's Mercantile. He counted them, found twenty-four afloat, and refocused his lenses. Within minutes, a fishing boat came into view—it was the *Hesperus*. Jim knew from marine records that it had been the vessel used by Merrill Goldwater before his license was revoked, so he waited. He was unable to make out who was in the *Hesperus's* wheelhouse, but he saw two young men hauling up the lobster pots and removing square bound packages. One of them had white- blond hair.

Jim smiled; he had his smugglers. The plan was never to tackle the team from another fishing boat, since Jim knew the suspect vessel would be outfitted with an engine which could outrun most anything of a similar size. However, a coast guard cutter was waiting off the horizon to give chase on his signal. He jumped down from the perch and engaged the *Nellie Bligh's* radio.

"Morning, 406, this is Sergeant Jim Cromwell, Royal Canadian Mounted Police, waiting on Captain Dale Farrington—over."

"Jim, hi, this is Dale. Thanks for giving us a heads up. You want to sign off here, or follow these clowns to Beantown—over."

"Hey, Dale, I'm a Mountie—gotta get my man. I'll keep off shore 'til they break, then they're all yours. I'll chopper down to Portland, so hold 'em 'til I get there. Watch your back, this guy's a pro. Good hunting—over."

"You got it, Jim, we're running long and slow, but as soon as they start south, I'll pick 'em up. Have a good day, see you later—out."

"USCG 406, *RCMP Nellie Bligh*, copy—over and out."

CHAPTER FOURTEEN

Merrill opened the *Hesperus's* throttle, and the seeming wreck of a vessel cut through the waves like a speedboat. Although the *Hesperus* encountered no other vessels on the run down to Zeb Cove, Merrill could feel the Coast Guard on his back. As he cut speed for his final approach, night was closing in. Merrill was unfamiliar with the area, but had a clear mental picture of the reefs, shoals, and eddies from his close study of the oceanographic charts. Slowing to a drift, he occasionally tickled the throttle to avoid getting too close to a rocky outcropping, and for several minutes, the *Hesperus* bobbed dark and silent in the shallow water.

Merrill's experienced eyes made out the shore and a jetty dead ahead, and while his paymaster's instructions were to wait for a signal light before berthing, at least one of the younger members of his crew became increasingly anxious. "Rake," rasped Merrill. "Stop dancing about, you're making me nervous."

"Can't help it," said Rake. "We're so close; just pull the goddamn boat in, why don't ya. I kin see the trucks up top. Dock this fucker, so I can haul ass." Rake hefted his forty-kilo load and paced nervously, waiting for the all clear.

"Like I said before," hissed Merrill. "We're waiting on the signal. You got everything straight in your mind?"

"Yeah."

"So tell me."

"Christ, how many times," snapped Rake. "What am I, a friggin' moron?"

"Just do it."

"Trucks is set ta go. We meet at Majestic Warehouse, Orient Heights, seven A.M. We git our money, rental is at the Shipwreck, and drive back ta Frenchman's. I'll get my fifty g's then."

"What about trouble?" asked Merrill.

"We's on our own. Ya know, old man, this is bullshit. We frig about here, we gonna get trouble. Fuck the signal—pull in or I's goin' over the side."

"Then you'll drown, you dumb shit. As it stands, the *Hesperus* is far enough out that if the cops show up I can turn on a dime, make a run out to sea, and dump the goods. I'm not risking everything by jumping the gun."

Rake took a step toward the rail. "Fuck it, I'm done waitin'. I'm goin'—"

"Wait," said Lance, grabbing Rake's backpack. "Look."

A light from the dunes flashed the all-clear.

As Merrill spat out the stogie he'd been chewing for the better part of an hour, he gently opened the throttle, and brought the *Hesperus* to the jetty. Rake was on the landing and running before Merrill turned off the engine.

When Merrill exited the wheelhouse, Lance was already to the dunes. But as the old man bent to pick up his bag, the throb of a large bore boat engine cut into the silence. Despite his sixty-plus years, he scurried over the side. He was barely a third of the way up the dock, when the area was flooded with light. "Lance," he panted. "Keep going, I'm right be—"

The men were caught dead center in a beam of light.

"U.S. Coast Guard. Attention men on shore, drop the bags, put your hands in the air, or we'll open fire. I repeat. Hands in the air, or we open fire."

• • •

Rake was near the trucks when he heard the voice from the ocean. He ignored it, repeating to himself, "on your own, on your own." And with adrenaline spiking, he sprinted the remaining yards to the closest vehicle. He hurled his bags in the truck bed and jumped in. The keys were in the ignition, the Dodge responded immediately, and he slammed the monster into drive. Then a piercing light beam from below pinpointed his position. It was at his back, and angled high, so he gunned the engine and peeled from the area amidst a maelstrom of sand, dirt, and pebbles.

The sluing Dodge burst from the headland, and Rake's hands jarred painfully as he encountered asphalt. But he hadn't gone ten yards with blacktop under spinning wheels when he dropped into a pothole. Pitching forward, he struck his temple on the steering wheel, and as he cursed, a shaft of red hot air zipped past his head. A bullet had come through the rear window to hang in the windshield like a fly in a web. Believing the gods were on his side, Rake let out a triumphant yell and punched a hole in the growing mosaic of the shattered windshield. A million silicate fragments exploded about him as the Dodge barreled forward.

Once he had clear view, Rake recognized his old stomping ground around Cape Elizabeth. He headed inland, confident that nobody would catch him this side of the White Mountains.

• • •

The others weren't so lucky. Merrill realized too late that twenty-five kilos at a run was more than the diminutive Lance had bargained for. And when shots hit his bags, Lance dropped them. Caught in the Coast Guard's beam of light, he clawed at the shifting sand and scrambled up the dunes. Then a bullet grazed his shoulder, and the impact spun him around and backwards, towards the water.

Merrill watched Lance tumble down the dunes and tried to stop his fall. The young man was too heavy—he hit the landing hard, and whipping around, clouted his leg on the jetty's upright. A sickening crack accompanied Lance's expletive.

"Get up," shouted Merrill to his stricken companion. "We've got to run! They're Feds out there."

"Ankle feels broken," said Lance, trying to stand. "Can't go any further. You keep going; I'll just hold you back."

Merrill dropped beside his lover. "I'm not leaving you; we're in this together."

"You have to go—now." Lance took the old man's hand and kissed it tenderly. "You have to, Big Daddy; who else is gonna post bail?"

"Can't do it, munchkin," whispered Merrill.

"For me, for us. I need you to get me out of this. I'll distract them—now go." Lance pushed Merrill forward, and screaming like a banshee, rolled further onto the jetty. As anticipated, the beam of light followed the blood-curdling noise, and gave the old man enough time to power his wiry sea legs up the dunes.

With tears streaming down his face, Merrill cursed every god he could think of and threw himself into a truck. Shots ripped into the rear tires before he felt the drag. But he wasn't going to let Lance's suffering be in vain. He locked his arms and held the stricken vehicle solid as it plunged into the darkness. As the tires shredded on asphalt and rim sparks illuminated the night, the old mariner had one goal: make the warehouse rendezvous, collect his money, and get Lance out of jail.

When the Dodge limped into an apartment house parking lot on the north side of Elizabeth Park with the transmission grinding and rims white hot, Merrill found cars aplenty. He hot-wired an open Toyota, and headed south.

•••

When the coast guard cutter's captain radioed Jim, he wasn't happy. "What happened?" asked Jim.

"It was a cluster fuck, Jim. God knows how these clowns outran us, but they did. Sorry."

"You get any of them?"

"We bagged one," said the captain. "A young guy, with four hold-alls of what looks like cocaine."

"They have help getting away?"

"There were trucks waiting for them. This stinks of the Albatross Alliance. Portland P.D. was patrolling and already got here. State's on the way. The one we have in custody got dinged. Bullet grazed his shoulder and he might have broken his ankle. Hang on … yeah, my C.P.O. confirms cocaine. The guy here isn't your Merrill. He's a mouthy, young turd with white hair. My shooter says the first guy who got away had a bunch of hold-alls and was also young. The second was definitely an old guy, and he's driving a truck with its tires shot out. Hey, Jim, sorry we couldn't come through for you. You'll have to get the others landside."

"Shit," barked Jim. "Okay, Dale, no problem. Told you Merrill is one slippery customer. Have Portland P.D. take the injured guy to Maine Medical; I'll talk to him there. Thanks for giving it your best shot. See you around. Over and out."

"Nellie Bligh, roger, later—over and out."

CHAPTER FIFTEEN

Jim was on frustrated automatic as he slowed to negotiate his cabin's driveway. On top of losing two of the three men involved in the drug pick-up, he hadn't heard from Sophie in a week. He'd left messages, and while he toyed with the idea of using his badge to call Granola Aviation and find out her schedule, he realized he was going to have to let her make the next move. He did, however, remember Mac mentioning Sophie's regular appearance in the tabloids and had indulged in a little creative snooping. After interrogating a couple of entertainment web sites, he discovered she was ferrying a rock group around the country. And over the next four days, the band was performing at the Portland Civic Center.

Jim walked into his kitchen to find his message light blinking. He hit the button and there she was.

"Hi Jim, its Sophie. I'm finally back in your neck of the woods. The kids I'm ferrying around have a four-night gig at the Civic Center. Would you have dinner with me? We need to talk about something. I'm at the Regent, usual room, 6B. Call me."

Jim immediately dialed her number.

"Captain Berg," said Sophie, all business.

"Sergeant Cromwell reporting for duty, Captain."

Sophie giggled. "Jim, hi. I'm so glad to hear you. Why didn't you call me before now?"

"Call you? I left three messages in Phoenix."

"Oops, my bad. I haven't been home, and with cell phones and all, I forget the old fashioned stuff."

"You have a cell?"

"Naturally. Didn't I give you the number?"

"*Sophie ...* "

"And here's me thinking you didn't want any more to do with me."

"Because you rejected me?" asked Jim. "For the record, I am not *that* guy. We are who we are, and not everything we do comes from a universal manual of life. That's why I'm pushing forty and still single. You're not the only one who chooses a job over a relationship."

"Talking about the job—how was the fishing expedition?"

"We got one guy, two got away. Frankly, it was a crap-shoot. But you know, the hell with work for now. I need to take a step back. So, how about we do some more of the drinks and conversation thing? I have a notion to sit on my deck listening to the loons."

"That sounds nice."

"I'm assuming the crew bus is still your primary means of transportation in Portland, so I'll come pick you up, say forty-five minutes?"

"Jim, be serious, I've flown coast to coast today. It's eight-thirty and I'm working on a minimum rest period. I'm about ready for bed."

"And your point?"

"You're not giving up, are you," said Sophie.

"Nope. Told you, when I see what I want, I go for it."

"I had tomorrow in mind, but what the hay, come and get me."

• • •

Was Sophie crazy or had Jim really just said he was setting aside work to be with her? And, even crazier, had she really said "what the hay" about getting a decent sleep between flights? She shook her head. Something was happening over which she had very little control, and she was perfectly all right with it.

Jim was waiting in the lobby when Sophie came from her room. "Well, Captain, again, you look stunning. If we can get down the front steps without being shot at, we have a good chance of making it back to my place."

They barely spoke on the drive to his cabin. Jim broke the silence as he switched off the engine. "Is everything okay? You're very quiet."

"I'm not accustomed to looking over my shoulder, and after all that's happened, being at the Regent was making me nervous."

"Nervous? That isn't like you. I can feel something else is on your mind."

"Amongst work things, you are."

Jim smiled. "Oh really?"

"I hope you have chardonnay chilled because about now you have me confused as to whether I'm coming or going."

"Does that mean I've made it onto the list of your life's priorities?"

"Your sarcasm is endearing. But I warn you. When I make up my mind about something, it's all or nothing."

Jim took her hand and kissed the knuckles. "Now that sounds like a challenge."

Sophie smiled. "Mr. Mountie, you have no idea."

• • •

Sophie was sitting on a deck chaise when Jim brought out wine and cheese. "It's beautiful here," she said. "So peaceful. I even heard that loon you mentioned. They sound so sad."

"Wait until you hear them at dawn."

"Pretty confident, aren't you?" said Sophie, taking a sip of wine.

"Hope springs eternal."

"You really have to stop that poetry thing. People will think you're a nut."

"As long as you don't, I'm good. That wine chilled enough?"

"It's perfect," said Sophie. "But before you get me sloshed, can I ask you something about work?"

"I'd rather talk about my elevated position on your priority list."

"I know, but if I don't get the business stuff off my chest, I'll bust."

"Okay, a small detour won't spoil the mood. I'm all ears."

Sophie giggled. "The mood? I just got here; there's a mood already?"

Jim ran his fingers down her arm. "Whenever you're around me, there's a mood."

"Could you set it aside for a few minutes?"

"I've been doing that for weeks. A bit longer won't hurt."

"Thank you," said Sophie. "I appreciate your restraint. So, after the Medellín fiasco, I got thinking about that Golden Lance Historical deal."

Jim smiled. "Wow, you're pretty tenacious when something's bothering you."

"Like a pit bull. Anyway, I found out the guy I was ferrying around is called Albert Ross. I was under contract to Albatross Marine and wondered why I was taking another job mid-contract. So, the only answer is that this Golden Lance guy, who happens to be called Albert Ross, has something to do with Albatross Marine."

"Excuse me?"

"Duh, Jim. Thought you were a hotshot. Albert Ross—*Albatross*. Granola wasn't making me double dip on a contract. I bet this Ross guy owns Albatross Marine. He was simply shipping machine parts he didn't want a competitor to know about."

Jim pulled Sophie close and pecked her on the nose. "You're a genius."

"Er, yeah ... why?"

"Give me a second; I have to call the office."

"Call the office? I thought this was our time?"

Jim pecked her on the nose again. "It will be, I promise. You just stumbled on a major connection in a list of characters I'm dealing with. I need to get Mac working on something. But you know, considering you and I were shot and we still don't know who did it or why, and stuff you shouldn't be involved in is popping up left and right, do you think it's wise to go poking around your company files?"

"Didn't poke around. Straight out asked the guy in Ops. I said Ross asked me out and I lost his number. He told me everything I wanted to know."

"You have Albert Ross's phone number?" asked an incredulous Jim.

"Sure. I tried it and got a recording. It's the old Albatross Marine in Illinois. So there's the definitive answer to one of the questions relating to that stuff you're so worried about."

Jim swiped a hand through his hair. "Sophie, look, I understand you're the kind of gal who needs to know what's going on. Coincidence bugs the hell out of me too. But you don't have all the facts. Have you considered that maybe you're entering dangerous territory?"

Sophie's smile radiated mischief. "Dangerous why? I simply needed to reassure myself that I wasn't ferrying around anything illegal. Now I know it was machine parts, I can move on."

Jim took her hand. "Please Sophie, promise me one thing."

"Which is?"

"You won't snoop around anymore. It's dangerous; you simply have to trust me on this. My job is putting together pieces of a puzzle, and you've stumbled into something you weren't supposed to."

"How do you work that out?"

"*Sophie* ... "

"There's that inflection again—what gives?"

"Don't make me get you any more involved."

"Involved?" asked Sophie. "Aren't I already involved? You can be as evasive as you like, but you're not fooling me. This is way bigger than my flying around machine parts, isn't it?"

Jim remained quiet.

"We're supposed to be friends. How can I trust you if you don't trust me?"

"All I can tell you is you're right. Machine parts are a tiny piece of the puzzle. Jesus. Sit still a minute; I really have to make that phone call."

As Jim entered the kitchen, he took a deep breath. With the introduction of Albert Ross, Sophie had stumbled upon a new link between Albatross Marine, Dante Goldwater Merrill, Lance Deveraux, and the drug pick up off the coast. He made his call and returned to the deck. "Sophie, I know this is weird, but I have to take you back to the Regent."

"Now? What prompted this?"

Jim had not wanted to tell Sophie his suspicions for fear her curiosity might place her in more jeopardy. However, he was now at a point where her not knowing could prove equally as dangerous. He took a deep breath. "You've connected pieces of a puzzle I've been working on for months. I'm now pretty convinced my being at the Regent at the same time as you was no coincidence. You told me you've irritated people since you joined Granola because you ask questions about who and what you fly about. I believe your digging around in company business got you shot. I haven't figured out if there's any connection between Granola and what I'm working on. However, I was at the Regent to watch a suspect that day, and my gut is telling me I was put there to get shot, too. Someone wants us both out of the way, and I don't think he'll give up until we're both out of the picture. Ergo, you are in danger and the best place for us to keep our eyes on you is at the hotel."

The blood drained from Sophie's face.

"Sophie, you're not going to like it, but I'm saying my piece." He took her hand and brought it to his heart. "You must know how I feel about you, and though you fight me every step of the way, I know you feel the same way about me. I care for you deeply and think we could have a future together."

"What about my—?"

His eyes hardened. "I want you out of Granola. I'm afraid for you there. I know you have a master plan for your life, but sometimes life doesn't go the way you planned. You can still fly but for someone else."

"But I—"

"Listen, darling, I'm not saying this as a cop—I'm saying it as a man. A man who very much wants you in his life. You need to get out of Granola before you're so deep into something illegal, I can't get you out. Will you give it some thought? For me ... for us? Please ... will you do that?"

Sophie ran her fingers down his face. "I think you need to know I'd do most anything for you."

CHAPTER SIXTEEN

Using every back-road he knew, Rake finally made it back to Victoria Falls. And as he approached his turn-off, he could hardly believe things had gone belly-up so fast. However, of one thing he was certain: the Coast Guard's beam had tagged his plate number, and he wasn't about to risk driving a marked vehicle to Boston. The circuitous route home had given him time to figure out what he needed to do. Coasting silently into the yard fronting his trailer, he transferred the hold-alls to his Ford, went into the house, and woke his wife.

"Wassup," Cele moaned. "Why ya waking me; ya know I don't sleep so good."

"Shut yer yap and put sumthin on."

"Jeez Louise," she said, flipping the night light. "Ya look like shit, what happened?"

"Nuthin, we're going out."

"Going out?"

"What are ya, a fucking parrot? What's there to eat?"

"Chips, pizza, what the hell?" Cele pulled on a robe.

Rake took a beer and cold pizza. "That all ya wearin'?"

"I didn't do laundry."

"Christ almighty, get in the truck and follow me."

"Follow you where?"

Rake lifted his hand as if to strike her.

"Okay, okay, don't have a cow, I'm on it." Cele waddled outside and squeezed herself behind the wheel of their old Ford.

Rake set off at a good clip, pointing the Dodge down a familiar logging road. He slowed several times for Cele to catch up, and when he finally stopped, he directed her to park. Then he maneuvered the Dodge to a rise running above an ancient excavation full of water.

Putting the truck in park, Rake got out and found a piece of wood to wedge against the accelerator. He made sure no rocks would impede forward motion, slipped the truck in neutral, and gave it a push. The brand new Dodge rolled gently forward, bobbled over the quarry lip, and sank beneath the murky water.

Cele was rubbing her belly as Rake yanked open the Ford's door. "Move over, ya fat bitch; I know where I'm going."

"Yeah, but where ya been? What's going on?"

"Nuthin'."

"Whose truck was that? It looked new."

"Dunno."

"Where we goin'?" asked Cele.

"I's goin' south," said Rake. "You is goin' back to bed."

"What if I wanna come with ya?"

"Ain't happnin'."

"It's a job, right? Waddaya do—rob a bank?"

"Better."

"How much better?" asked Cele.

"Enough."

• • •

As she heard the old Ford pull away, Cele knew Rake had been up to no good. However, she was confident he'd be back at least one more time with whatever money he was being paid. Then she would strike. Wiseass thought he called the shots. Not this time. As she downed a beer, Cele formulated how to divest the horny weasel of his money.

CHAPTER SEVENTEEN

The sun was rising as Rake pulled cautiously up to the warehouse in Orient Heights. There was no sign of life, but as he slowly circled the building, he noticed a Toyota sedan with someone asleep inside. He turned off his engine and coasted silently alongside. Merrill was fast asleep. Quietly leaving the Ford, Rake positioned himself beside the old man and, smiling sadistically, thumped his fist as hard as he could on the roof.

Instantly awake, Merrill's head snapped back. "Fuckin' stupid moron, I could've had a heart attack."

"I coulda bin the cops. Where's the money guy?"

Merrill checked his watch. "Ten minutes, asshole. You don't even have a watch?"

Rake could see nothing on the rear seat of the car. "Where's ya stuff?"

"Didn't make it."

"And Lance?"

"Feds got him."

Rake smiled. "Shiiiiat. So I's the only one wi' money comin'."

A frown crossed Merrill's face.

"Ya know, old man, I bin thinkin'. I got forty k o' snow here—that's a shitload o' green on the street. Why the fuck am I gettin' a lousy fifty grand?"

"'Cos that's what was agreed. Don't get any ideas about messing with me or New York."

Rake pulled the hold-alls to the side of his truck bed. "I guess fifty's better'n zip."

"Waddaya mean—we split the fifty."

"Don't think so," said Rake.

"They're not gonna deal with a piece o' crap like you."

"They'll deal wi' whoever's holdin' the dope, old man."

Before Merrill could answer, a BMW swooped into the parking lot and pulled up beside them. A black on black minder unfurled from behind the wheel, walked around the car, and opened the rear door.

Alligator boots preceded a suit in designer sunglasses, and manicured fingernails flicked a toothpick across the parking lot. "Gentlemen," the man said. "You have my merchandise?"

Rake lifted the handle on one of the hold-alls. "Got mine."

The minder let down the Ford's tailgate, reached forward, and lifted the hold-alls as if they were bags of donuts. He released the zipper on each, removed one of the tightly bound bundles, and slit a fingertip-sized gash in the side. Wetting a pinky, he tasted the merchandise and nodded to alligator boots. Then the mountain of a black man re-zipped the hold-alls, transferred them to the Beemer's trunk, and stood next to his boss.

"This is thirty-five G, tops," said alligator boots.

"Seems we got us a misunderstanding here," said Rake, casting an enquiring look at Merrill. "That snow worth way more 'an thirty-five. We had an agreement."

"We?" asked alligator boots.

Merrill smiled knowingly and shook his head.

"Okay, y'all an' Merrill here. But seems if I did the run, I hauled the goods, an I kep' my end o' the bargain, I deserve—"

The minder unbuttoned his jacket and placed a hand deliberately beneath his arm.

"Mr. Black here," said alligator boots, "seems to see things a little differently."

Rake was not so foolhardy as to attempt anything, knowing the huge man's bulk concealed a gun. "So when do I get paid?"

Alligator boots shook out the handkerchief artfully wedged in his breast pocket, removed his sunglasses, and wiped non-existent *schmutz* from the lenses. "Where's the rest of my merchandise?"

Merrill coughed nervously. "Feds were waitin'—they got it."

Several uncomfortable seconds of silence accompanied alligator boots's lens cleaning. "Fortunately for both of you, my contact already told me that." Replacing his glasses, he shook out the handkerchief and slipped it back into his pocket. Then, gesturing two fingers to his minder, alligator boots got back in the BMW.

The minder removed two bundles of notes from a valise in the trunk and lobbed them at Rake.

"Hold on, this ain't thirty-five," said Rake, flipping the wads. "It's like twenty. Where the rest?"

The rear window slide silently open and alligator boots smiled sardonically. "Where my trucks?"

As the BMW sped away leaving them in its dust, Rake turned on Merrill. "What's this horse-shit deal?" he yelled. "I risk my life for a lousy twenty grand? How long that gonna last?"

"Ten."

"Ten what? If ya think I's givin' ya any of this, ya can kiss my ass."

Merrill moved toward Rake.

"One step closer, old man, and as tough as ya think y'ar, I'll kill ya where ya stand." He peeled off some notes and threw them at Merrill. "Thanks for nuthin'."

Merrill let the money fall to the ground. "Jerking me around is not a good idea."

Rake hoisted a finger, got in his truck, and headed back to Maine.

CHAPTER EIGHTEEN

As Sophie paced, her anxiety built. She'd agreed to remain in her hotel room when Jim asked because she quite often stayed in her room for hours when she was on a layover. But now that she realized she was confined, the walls were closing in on her. Just a few hours was driving her mad.

She also understood why Jim had only been able to stay a few minutes. After all, the sooner he solved his case, the sooner she'd be free. But not having him near was different now. Despite what she'd first thought about his cavalier attitude toward life, she was wrong. He was nothing like the jerks she had dated. He was deeper and more grounded. His words and actions were leagues more sincere than those of any man she'd ever met, and, despite her reservations, she realized she cared for him as much as he did for her.

Caring for someone in such a way was a new emotion for Sophie, and she found it confusing, frightening, and blissfully satisfying all at once. But she could no longer deny it. Something intangible radiated from Jim Cromwell. And that something seeped into her very soul and gave her peace. She had thought working at a job she loved was satisfying enough and believed she was monumentally lucky to be living her dream. But it was all so much smoke and mirrors, and now she was alone in a nightmare—a nightmare only she could dispel.

She had been such a fool. A fool with an ego that blinded her to what really mattered. Life wasn't about her career. Life was about when she could next be with him, look into his eyes, and hear him say he cared. Without him near, emptiness consumed her. It had been a matter of hours, but she so wanted Jim around to explain what was happening and to reassure her that while caution was necessary, she wasn't really in danger.

But in her heart, she knew Jim would not needlessly put her through that. She also knew that they were both free spirits who had a hard time with boundaries, which was why on his visit to Phoenix he said he'd wait for her to make the next move. It was time. The only way she could truly feel safe was to be in his life.

"We could have a future together," he'd said, and the thought made her soar. Sophie picked up the phone and called Granola. Then she called Jim. "Can you come back to the Regent for a few minutes?" she said. "We need to talk."

• • •

Within minutes, Jim was at her door, concerned. He pecked her on both cheeks. "Has something happened?"

"You might say that. Can you stay a while?"

He could see how upset she was. "Sure, I left Mac working on something which doesn't need me. What gives?"

"You can't lock me in this hotel room for four days."

"Sophie, we talked about this. I'm going to do whatever it takes to protect you. The guard and the locked door stay."

"Well let me disabuse you of that notion right now. Don't you have something called a 'safe house'?"

Jim smiled. "We do. It still involves confinement, but the guard is usually inside the door."

"Oh. In that case, if I'm in line for that kind of protection, I can't think of any better place than with you."

"With me, at work?"

She gave him *the look*. "You live in a friend's cabin in the boonies. Nobody but the Portland P.D. knows you live there. What could be safer?"

"You mean you want to stay with me at the cabin?"

"That's precisely what I mean."

"It's got one bedroom. I don't have the space to accommodate—"

"You have a bed?"

Jim nodded.

"And a shower with running water, preferably hot?"

Jim smiled.

"I presume you have food, and I know you have liquor. What more do I need? Unless you just don't want me to stay with you."

Jim pulled her close. "You know that's absurd. I do, very much. What I don't want is for you to think I'm taking advantage of you and the situation."

Sophie smiled. "What situation? Jim, please, I'm not as naïve as you seem to think. Since the minute I was shot, I knew I might have stepped into something I shouldn't. I told you, I make waves. In fact, I was hoping when I told you about Albert Ross you'd brush it off and say 'how nice, mystery solved, have some more cheese.' The mere fact you didn't, and you exhibited that tell of yours—"

"Tell?" asked Jim. "What tell?"

"When you get worried about something you say *Sophie* with this sort of quizzical inflection. It's happened half a dozen times. And I bet you also have a tickling in the back of your neck, or an eye twitch, though I haven't seen one yet."

"*Sophie* ... "

"Ah-ha, there it is," said Sophie smugly. "Frankly, a degree in psychology pretty much lets me say, 'been there, done that, got the t-shirt.'"

Jim smiled. "You have an answer for everything, don't you?"

"Not so. I don't have an answer for why you don't fully trust me. I know you can't talk about your cases, but at some point real friends have to cross a line. I'm ready to do that. And the mere fact that my reference to Albert Ross spooked you, as did my recalling the platinum blond, means we both have to be clued in on certain things if we're going anywhere together."

"And right now, where would you like to go together?"

Sophie smiled. "I called Granola and told them they would have to send in a replacement because my shoulder was acting up. I took four days sick leave and told them I'd make my own way back to Phoenix to see my doctor. That gives me time to get to know you better and see if we really do have a future together."

"You think we can do that in four days?"

"I thought I was supposed to be the one fighting *you* every step of the way. If we belong together, it will take a few hours of living together to find that out."

" *Touché*. So when did this revelation take place?"

"The minute you walked out that door. I missed you."

"Ah-ha, little ol' irresistible me," teased Jim. Then he pulled her into his arms and kissed her.

• • •

Sophie was staring out over the cabin's acreage as Jim came up behind her.

"I really love this place," she said. "Do you think the Neversons would sell it to me?"

"They wouldn't sell it to me, so I'd say probably not."

"Pity, I can really see myself living here."

Jim smiled. "For the next few days you will be. However, me being me, I have to know."

"Know what?"

"Back at the hotel, you said I didn't trust you because 'real' friends would cross a line."

"Umm."

"It's not that I don't trust you per se, but sometimes what you know can get you into trouble. I don't want to give you information which might harm you or if passed to the wrong person, might compromise the investigation."

"I get that," said Sophie. "As it seems I may already be guilty of that."

"You also said you're ready to cross the line, and I don't think you were talking about trust."

Sophie turned to face him. "Absolutely right, Mr. Detective. I was talking about us."

"Oh?" asked Jim.

"Despite what you may think, I haven't been fighting you. I seem to attract jerks like a magnet and was simply being cautious because I didn't want to get involved with another one."

"So can I safely assume I'm out of the jerk range?"

"You can. And me being me, in crossing the line mode, I have to know." Sophie pulled him by his belt. "Come here." She kissed him passionately.

"I really like the crossing the line stuff," said Jim, his voice husky with desire.

"You ain't seen nothin' yet." Sophie unbuckled Jim's belt, released his zipper, and placed her hand inside his pants.

He smiled. "That makes your line quite clear."

"Good," said Sophie. "So take off your clothes."

It was unusual for Jim to be on the receiving end of such an aggressive sexual advance, and he found the situation intoxicating. "Right here, on the deck in front of the world?"

Sophie giggled. "It's getting dark—who but the deer is going to see us?"

•••

Lit only by moonlight, they shucked clothes where they stood. Each knew why they were there, and there were no mind games being played. Clinging together, body fused to deliciously sensitive body, his erection lay hard against her belly. He was, without doubt, the most blatantly erotic man Sophie had ever encountered, and when he softly bit her neck and shoulders, she was irretrievably lost. Sophie barely noticed when he backed her to the wall, his breathtaking kisses accompanying fingers circling her navel. And after his fingers explored her deep inside and his penis pushed into her, she gasped. He seemed considerably larger than anyone she remembered, and his thrusting flowed like liquid, high and full in her belly. She was almost as tall as he was and assumed their standing had caused his unexpected depth. And when he told her to relax her knees and bear down on him, the shock made her cry out. Jim's rhythm continued to caress the unimaginable depths of her being, hitting receptors like never before. She was hovering on the edge of reason, melting around his body. And when the cadence in her womb blossomed into overwhelming ecstasy, she cried. But her tears were not from pain. Her feelings were much, much deeper. They were primal, animal, and imbued her with a need to love him with every fiber of her being. She wanted to be the only woman he wanted—to let him know she would be his forever. And when his tongue plunged deep into her throat, she climaxed like never before.

•••

Jim woke to the smell of coffee and the mournful cry of the loons echoing around the lake. From bed, he could see Sophie leaning on the deck railing, her shapely legs ending at the rounding of her bare butt. And when a breeze rippled her cotton shirt, transparent as gossamer in the morning sun, he remembered her athletic body, as elegant during the previous night's action as it now was in repose. Swinging his legs from the huge bed, he moved into the bathroom, cinched a towel around his waist, and padded to the kitchen. He poured two mugs of coffee, added half-and-half, and joined her.

Sophie apparently didn't immediately hear Jim approach, because when he said "good morning," she turned with the startled look of a deer frozen in the headlights.

He pushed a mug in her direction. "Sorry, force of habit; I hope you take it white."

Her smile said she did, and, kissing her cool-morning fingertips, she reached across and touched them to his forehead. "Thank you; any coffee not brewed on an airplane is good with me."

"Why did you let me sleep?"

"Looked like you needed it."

"Haven't slept that well in some time."

"Vigorous exercise will do that."

Jim grinned. Sophie had put him through a workout the night before, and he felt drained. Not the wearying kind—the adrenaline pumping, heart stopping, megawatt electric, fantastic sex kind. "Thank you," he whispered, brushing a hand down her arm.

"For what?" She sipped her coffee.

"Being you, being here, crossing the line."

"You're welcome."

He liked the way she said, "you're welcome." It wasn't the typical American reflex action. It was more sincere somehow, like she'd actually decided to say it. "So," he said, moving in close. "Any second thoughts about our impetuosity last night?"

"None, what about you?"

"Zip, nada, nothing." Jim set both their mugs on the railing. Then, encircling her with muscular arms, he nuzzled her neck. "So, I'll call the office and tell them I'll be out today. Maybe we can go back to bed?"

Sophie smiled. "I'm not tired."

"Neither am I."

"Well, well, Mr. Mountie, it's nice to know you're not all business. Sophie put a hand on his heart. "There's an out-of-control beast in there after all."

"I could say the same about you." Jim brushed his lips across hers. "Sophie, I've been thinking—"

"Uh oh, that doesn't sound good from a newly resurrected beast."

Jim smiled. "Once you go back to work, I don't want anyone to know about us. It might put you in more danger and could really compromise my investigation."

"Don't worry, I'm keeping you all to myself. Besides, if the media got wind of a romance, you'd be all over the tabloids right alongside me."

"Jeez, I'd forgotten about that side of your life."

"Second thoughts now, I bet?"

"Nope," answered Jim. "Now stop talking and follow me."

"Thought you had to call your office."

"They can wait, I can't."

Sophie grinned as Jim led her back to bed.

CHAPTER NINETEEN

Sophie was making sandwiches when Jim came out of the shower. "Couldn't find much," she said. "You bachelors must eat out a lot."

"Occupational hazard," said Jim, toweling water from his hair. "By the way, you mentioned hot water. Don't get second position in the shower line; the water is lukewarm."

"Good to know. Next time, we bathe together."

Jim came behind her and nuzzled her neck. "Dang, you're killing me here. So what do you want to do this afternoon?"

"This afternoon? Don't you have an investigation to run?"

"I can take a day off, too."

"Wow, we really are crossing some lines here. Does this place have acreage?"

"Yeah, fifteen."

"It's so beautiful; can we take a walk around?"

"I have a better idea. Do you ride?"

Sophie's eyes twinkled. "You tell me."

"*Sophie* ... "

She laughed aloud. "Oh, you mean a *horse*. I have been known to."

"My friend, who owns this place, has a farm up the road. Shall I call him and borrow a couple?"

"Sounds like fun, but what about riding clothes? I at least need jeans."

"There's women's stuff in the bottom drawer of the dresser."

Sophie gave him "the look."

"Stop with your nonsense. They belong to my friend's wife. Remember, I'm just borrowing this place for a while. She's as tall as you and about the same ... " Jim hands motioned a woman's curves. "Well, you know. I'm sure she won't mind."

• • •

Within the hour, Jim and Sophie were leaving Mark Neverson's yard atop a couple of horses.

"So where are we going?" asked Sophie.

"We'll stick to the logging trails and then swing by a couple of Mark's quarries, which are really beautiful this time of year."

"You know these woods well then."

"Only from maps. They've been part of my case research for weeks. It'll be fun to see them for real."

"Yikes, what if we get lost?"

Jim pulled out his phone. "Backup."

They had been riding for nearly an hour when Jim turned to Sophie. "Branches get a bit low here, so watch out. We're coming to a quarry Mark's family attempted to mine, but the dig kept flooding."

"Are there many quarries?"

"Mark has at least a dozen on his land, but then he does own everything for miles around."

"All this space must be nice," said Sophie. "I love the climate in Phoenix, but it's so crowded now."

"So move out here."

"I go where there's an airport. You couldn't even land a chopper in these trees."

Halfway along a winding trail, the horses entered an offshoot going up a rise. They stopped at the edge of a water-filled excavation. And while Jim expected to show Sophie something of the beauty of the abandoned quarry, it was marred by the back end of a truck sticking out of the water. "Good grief," he said. "What happened here?"

"Could someone else have come up for a look and gone over the edge?" asked Sophie.

"It could've been here weeks."

"Don't think so," said Sophie, gesturing down. "Those tire tracks are pretty new."

"Wow, that campfire girl training came in useful after all."

"Quit the sarcasm, mister. Someone might be in there. Look—the plate doesn't have a loon on it."

"That's because it's Massachusetts."

"And that means?"

Jim called Mac. "Yeah, Mac, black Dodge. Okay, get everybody together at Mark Neverson's. I'll warn him."

After speaking to Mark's wife, Jim pocketed his phone. "Rats," he said.

"What's going on?" asked an impatient Sophie.

"Turns out I've been looking for this vehicle."

"You as in *the police*?"

"Remember when I was in Phoenix; I said I had to leave to go fishing?"

"And I teased you about goofing off."

Jim smiled. "I was following smugglers. This was one of the vehicles used in their getaway."

"So I guess that means our leisurely ride is over?"

"Sorry about that," said Jim. "Now, can you really ride? 'Cos we're gonna have to pick up the pace. Mark was out and his wife couldn't identify the quarry from my description. We have to go back, so I can guide the team back here."

"Okay, I'm following you. Let's go."

CHAPTER TWENTY

The volunteer fire brigade's ancient engine was first to arrive at the farm. Local farmhands who made up the rescue team followed. Limerick Towing pulled in with an assortment of tavern rats and anyone else up for an adventure, and the state troopers, who'd been miles from the scene, arrived last. Mark Neverson and his wife, J.P., were there to greet their friends and neighbors and recall the last bit of excitement they'd had—when one of Bill Sharp's heifers sank to its neck in the Clemons Pond swamp.

Sophie simply stared in surprise. It appeared as if half the town had turned out to help.

As Sophie handed off the horses to a farmhand, Mark's wife joined her.

"Hi," she said. "I'm J.P. Neverson. You must be the pilot Jim told us about."

Sophie held out her hand. "Yes, Sophie Berg. I thought we were supposed to keep a low profile. With this crowd, I think that's pretty much a bust."

"Don't worry about that. Folks are here for a dose of excitement. Unless you spontaneously combust, they won't even notice you. Mark and I don't count. We're as close as Jim has to family in these parts. The jeans look good on you."

"Thank you," said Sophie. "I hope you don't mind me commandeering them?"

"Not a bit," said J.P. "They were tight on me, so I never wore them. Shall I give you a ride back to the cabin?"

"I thought I might go with Jim."

J.P. shook her head. "He's in full Mountie mode now. It's best you write him off for a couple of days."

Sophie raised an eyebrow. "Is that usual?"

"It is. When Jim's working, he's totally single-minded. You'll be alone at the cabin. Did he show you all the films, music, books—where he keeps the booze?"

"Well actually, apart from booze, we, er, didn't get around to that sort of entertainment."

J.P. laughed aloud. "He's impossible. I bet you know where the bed is though."

Sophie blushed.

"Sorry, didn't mean to tease," said J.P. "Jim is like my kid brother. I sometimes forget he's allowed a grown-up life. When I drive you back, I'll show you where everything is. Does he have food?"

"Bread and cold cuts."

"Typical man. He invites a friend over and doesn't even get provisions in."

"Does he invite friends a lot?" asked Sophie.

"No. I nag him all the time to get some company, but it falls on deaf ears. Most gals can't cope with him working all hours God sends. In fact, when he told us he had a special friend, I'd have bet money on him adopting a puppy. Come on up to the house—I'll put together enough food to keep you going until he gets back."

•••

It was ten-thirty when Jim called the cabin. "Hi, you. I'm so sorry; this took longer than I thought."

"Where are you now?"

"Back in Portland, at the police department."

"Are you coming back tonight?"

"I don't think so. I have reports, and I'm waiting for forensics. I also have a guy I need to question about—"

"You don't have to explain. It's your job; I understand."

"Will you be all right alone?"

"Absolutely. J.P. gave me food and showed me where everything is. I love this 'Winnie in the Wilderness' thing. I have homemade blackcurrant and apple pie, *a la mode* no less, and a very nice bottle of chardonnay. What have you got?"

"Cold pizza and root beer."

"Ah-ha. That'll teach you for running out on a gal after you had your wicked way with her."

"I didn't mean to—"

"I know," said Sophie. "Look, as you'll be tied up from here on out, maybe I should scoot back to Phoenix."

"You know, Sophie, I've been thinking. Maybe it's not such a good idea for you to go back to work at all."

"I guess you like living with me thus far?"

Jim laughed. "I like it just fine."

"So don't rush me, Jim. I've a lot more soul-searching to do. What happened today? Any bodies?"

"No, we winched out the vehicle and found nothing. But the cab's rear window and windshield were blown out, so we know it was the first of two vehicles that ran from us in Zeb Cove recently. We have one person from that fiasco in custody; he's the one I'll be questioning. Are you sure you're all right there alone?"

"Jim, I'm a pilot. I fly all over the country and stay alone in hotels all the time. I'm a big girl; I don't need a man around."

"*Sophie …* "

"Okay, so I might need one man around, but I can wait. Just be careful out there. Will you call me again tonight?"

"What do you think?"

CHAPTER TWENTY-ONE

When Jim received the Dodge's forensic report, he smiled. It seemed the body of the truck had yielded nothing usable in the way of prints—probably due to its immersion in the murky, silt-filled water—however, the partially submerged tailgate yielded a clear set of prints. The prints were identical to those found on the *Hesperus* and confirmed the identity of the third smuggler at Zeb Cove.

"Hey, Mac," Jim said into the police band radio. "The prints pulled from the truck belong to Richard Jensen, that survivalist dude we're looking for. Did we have any luck pinning down his location?"

"Green trailer on the right, backwoods, Maine?"

"Very cute, Mac, but it's singers we need, not comedians. Jensen's rap sheet says he does most anything for a buck—yard work, logging, day labor at Portland Jetport. Your brother-in-law was helpful last time; can you get back onto him, see if he knows anything useful? And Mac ... "

"I know. Be discreet."

•••

Within an hour, Mac was back on the radio to Jim. "Okay, Jim, I got good news and bad news."

"Give it to me," said Jim.

"Good news is my brother-in-law is very familiar with Richard Jensen. He's a local hot head who thinks he's a ladies' man. Causes weekend mayhem tackling the out-of-towners' wives, but apparently he got adventurous a while back and hit on my sister. It got ugly."

"You didn't know about that?"

"Neither of 'em said a word to me. There was talk around town about *someone* hitting on gals from out of town, but had I known he was trying that crap on my sis, it would have pushed ugly to a whole new level. And not for nothing but our Richard Jensen could be a dangerous good-old-boy in other ways. Don't know whether his record mentions it, but some say he was Special Forces; knows his way around weapons and explosives."

"Don't all those militia types?"

"Pretty much, but not usually on Uncle Sam's dime. Anyway, when he tackled my sis, bro-in-law saw the wrong end of Jensen before his wife, Cele, dragged him into a truck and drove off."

"This going somewhere, Mac?"

"The wife called him *Rake*."

"Oh yeah," said Jim. "It's all about connecting the dots Mac, and those dots lead us to the Jetport. What's the bad news?"

"The Jetport," said Mac. "Seems after out last raid, Jensen was offered full-time work at the warehouse, stuck it one day, and then called in sick. Hasn't been seen since."

"So?" asked Jim. "Isn't that the nature of day laborers? For whatever reason, they can't hold down a regular job. We'll just monitor the warehouse until he shows."

"Ordinarily, I'd agree. However, it doesn't jive that given the chance at the weekly guarantee, which I assume he'd use to make meth and sell on, that he'd blow it off?"

"Only one thing would make a guy do that," said Jim. "More money."

"That was my thought too."

"Did you find out from the Jetport where he lives?"

"That's more bad news," answered Mac. "Nobody has a clue. Beezer Trucking is pretty loose with the day laborers; generally, all they get for an address is a post office box. However, I've been thinking—"

"Dangerous concept, Mac."

"Yeah, I love you, too. Jensen has done some casual logging and while they usually rotate around the farms here, true woodsmen are different. They're outside the mainstream and live like hermits."

"That we know," said Jim. "What's your point?"

"These guys could be hunkered a yard away from you, and you'd never see them. So we need help from someone who knows the backwoods as well as—if not better than—the survivalists do. I can only think of one person, and he's a friend of yours."

"Mark Neverson?"

"The very same."

"Thanks, Mac, I'll call him."

• • •

"You had any experience with survivalists?" asked Jim.

"I pick up an occasional trap," said Mark. "But I've never actually seen a person. I don't tolerate traps of any kind, and they usually stay off my land. I do know where a couple of old boys have been living rough, but if they leave me and mine alone, they can set a while."

"You own and farm most of the land around her, so I assume you spend a lot of time checking boundaries and such. If I brought you forestry maps, could you put in the trails and encampments not shown?"

Mark smiled. "I could, but if you try to find them, you'd be up a creek once you got on the ground. It all looks the same to an outsider; you'd be lost in ten minutes."

"I worked out how to get to and from the quarry."

"Beginner's luck," said Mark. "And the quarry you were at is not far in. The trails go back miles."

"That's why I need your help."

"You helped my family with a law enforcement issue; it's the least I can do. Besides, there's not much going on at the farm," said Mark. "And I know J.P. is itching to find out more about your lady friend. Bring over the maps."

A text message vibrated Jim's phone, and he looked at the screen. It simply said: HELP and was signed, *Sophie*.

CHAPTER TWENTY-TWO

"Sophie, it's Jim, what's happening?"

"Thank God you called back. Where are you?"

"Portland—what's wrong? Er, I got up late, had coffee on the deck, and then I thought, it's such a lovely morning, why don't I take a walk in the woods. Might be nice to stretch my legs—"

"*Sophie* … "

"Sorry, I'm a little shaken, trying to remain calm—someone just shot at me!"

"In the cabin?"

"No. In the woods."

"Did you have the orange vest on like I said?"

"Yes. A blind man could have seen me in that thing."

"Were you off trail?" asked Jim.

"No. I went exactly where you took me before—down the logging trail and past the cemetery. I'd just rounded that big stand of pines on the right when I came across a guy winching a deer into the back of a pick-up. The gal with him just up and fired a gun at me."

"Are you in the cabin?"

"I'm in the cellar where J.P. keeps her canned goods."

"Good. That's actually a gun locker. Do you see the shotgun on the rack above the door?"

"What am I supposed to do with that?"

"There's no lock on the inside, so you point it at the door and anyone tries to come in before I get there, you pull the trigger."

"Good God, is it loaded? I don't know anything about guns."

"Sophie, look, I can jump in a chopper and be there in twenty minutes. I'm going to tell you how to put cartridges in that thing, and you will move to the back corner of the locker and hunker down 'til I get there. I'll call Mac and see if he's in the area, but make no mistake, if somebody opens that door, you will fire the gun. Do you understand me?"

"Yes. Tell me how to work this thing and get the hell in that chopper."

Jim told Sophie how to break the gun and put in the cartridges and then called Mac. "Where are you?"

"Outside the Donut Hole in Limerick."

"Okay, you're less than ten minutes from my place. Get over there now."

"Thought I was picking up Sophie this afternoon?"

"Someone is shooting at her."

"Jesus H. Christ, I'm on the way."

"Mac, go in hot," said Jim. "Scaring off our shooter is good enough right now. And don't go near the gun locker in the cellar. Sophie has a twelve bore trained on the door. I'll see you in twenty."

• • •

As the chopper hovered above the cabin's vegetable patch, Jim jumped out. Mac was out of his cruiser armed with his shotgun. He jogged towards Jim. "All quiet, boss. Circled the house, it all seems intact. Haven't heard any vehicles and no one came out the woods or down the trail."

Jim nodded towards the shotgun. "Big guns, I see."

"Got more chance of hitting something in these woods. Did Sophie just disturb some hunters?"

"Don't know yet, but as we've both been in somebody's sights already, best be safe than sorry." Jim and Mac walked into the house and stood to the side of the gun locker door. "Sophie, it's Jim. I'm coming in. Is that okay?" He waited a few seconds. "Sweetie, click the safety on the gun, and let me know it's okay to come in."

Sophie opened the door and smiled. "Jeez, what did you think I'd do, shoot you?"

Jim took the gun and handed it to Mac. "We never know how a person will react under pressure. I momentarily forgot you're the drug kingpins' hot shot pilot of choice."

"Very funny," she said, pecking Jim on the cheek. "Good to see you. So who the hell shot at me?"

"Not sure. Mac said he couldn't see anyone about. Maybe you simply disturbed a hunter. Locals know Mark doesn't hold with hunting, so it could have been an out-of-towner."

"They didn't look like hunters, out-of-town or otherwise. No vests, no dogs, just a good looking dude in jeans and a t-shirt, and a very pregnant young woman."

"Oh really," said Jim. "How about we go upstairs and get some details. Hey, Mac, thanks for responding so fast. Why don't you secure that gun and get back to whatever. I'll work the rest of the day from here as I have to get Mark's input on my forestry maps."

Mac nodded. "You got it. Good to see you again, Sophie."

She smiled and started up the cellar stairs. "You too, Mac, thanks for being there."

Jim joined Sophie in the living room. "Now, Miss Intrepid, let's have the details from the top."

"As I said, I was out walking and came across this couple. He was loading a deer into the back of his truck; she had the gun."

"Describe him."

"Tall, early thirties. Dark and sort of dangerous looking, Gypsy-king type. Like one of those guys you see on a romance novel cover."

"That's the same description Mac's sister gave us for one Richard 'Rake' Jensen."

"And he is?"

"Local survivalist and meth dealer we want to speak to."

"Good grief, sounds like a peach. And it seems you may have found him," said Sophie.

"I'm betting he's long gone into the backwoods, so he won't be easy to flush out. You said the girl was young and heavily pregnant?"

Sophie nodded.

"That's probably his wife."

"She didn't look a day over fifteen and could barely lift up the gun to fire it," added Sophie. "Thank God she wasn't much of a shot, or I'd be a goner."

Jim ran his fingers down Sophie's cheek. "You're remarkably calm about all this. Are you really all right?"

"Sure, why do you ask?"

"I don't think I've ever had a girlfriend who took what I do in stride."

"It's your job," said Sophie. "I knew what I bargained for when I decided to get involved with you."

"The others did, too. I guess they didn't care enough about me to put up with it."

"Sounds like you had a bad experience."

"My last relationship. There was the usual assortment of mayhem, I got injured, and she wanted me to give up being a Mountie."

"Did she get shot?"

Jim smiled. "No, she was just scared out of her wits a couple of times."

"What a wuss. Hopefully you pointed out that unless she gets shot, she needs to get a grip."

Jim smiled. "That's my girl."

"I gotta say, though, being your other half has its downside."

Jim looked sad. "That mean you're going to bail on me?"

"Did she?"

"Yup, all the way back to Germany."

"Well don't worry; I'm made of tougher stuff. I might be off to all points North America, but at some point, I'll make my way back to you. Because much against my better judgment, I'm a little bit nuts about you and am more than prepared to put up with whatever *it* is. Now before I have to once again fly off into the unknown, I will need to inspect the goods I have recently bargained for. When I return, I will then be able to assess if the baggage I have taken on has sustained further damage."

"I'm just *baggage*, eh?"

Sophie smiled. "At the moment, you are correct. However, I am reserving the right to elevate you to a permanent possession. In the meantime, Sergeant, you'll need to come with me—that's an order."

Jim grinned. "Yes, ma'am. Who am I to argue with a captain?"

CHAPTER TWENTY-THREE

Jim Cromwell paced the floor of the Portland Police Department waiting for a phone call. He'd received information from forensics that not only had a set of prints belonging to Dante Goldwater Merrill been lifted from the stolen Toyota they'd recovered at a warehouse in Orient Heights, but also that casts made of another vehicle at the scene revealed High-Grade Z-Rated Yokohama tires imported through Akron, Ohio. And while that information in itself might not have proved damaging to anyone, Jim had found out the factory had distributed the expensive custom tires to only fifteen U.S. outlets—and one of them happened to be Kickin' It Custom in Queens, New York. He fancied he now had a direct path from Maine to his drug distributor.

When the phone rang, it was the NYPD, who said Kickin' It Custom had been on their watch list for months. However, though they had an informant in place, they could find nothing to tie the operation to anything illegal. All they could tell Jim was the high-end car dealership pandered to the rich and famous. And to gain access to the showroom and speak to anyone, a customer referral was needed. Jim put down the phone and smiled. He knew exactly who might get that referral.

...

"Well hello, Sergeant Cromwell," said Sophie. "Where have you been for the past two days?"

"Pulling impossibly late nights to try and forget how much I need you. What else would I be doing? I'm glad to see you're still off the flying roster; I guess your plan worked."

Sophie giggled. "You should have seen my performance at the doctor's office. I could have won an Oscar. For the foreseeable future, I'm on PR duty only. You know I loathe all that stuff, but if being so visible makes me less of a target, and you get to sleep at night, I'm okay with it."

"Who says I sleep at night? I'm alone and don't seem to manage that so well anymore."

"Don't fret, little boy; mama will be home soon."

Jim laughed. "So, I've been monitoring you in the tabloids. Who was the bozo at the *Gargantua* premiere?"

"*Oooo*," she giggled. "Is that a little green monster raising its ugly head?"

"Maybe a tiny, tiny one. By the way, I loved the navy blue Badgley Mischka you wore, and the emeralds were a touch of genius."

"Well thank you, kind sir. It's good to know you have a keen fashion sense. Never know when that might come in handy."

"Yeah that's me, a positive Mr. Blackwell," said Jim. "So who was the bozo practically drooling over you?"

Sophie laughed. "Before or after the flick?"

"Before—penguin suit, glasses, slicked back hair."

"That was Skipper. Real name Cecil Calhoun Purvis the third."

"Good grief, are you serious?" asked Jim.

"Swear to God. He's the nephew of one of Granola's major shareholders and heads up PR and Marketing. I didn't wear it, but he bought me a wrist corsage."

"How sweet, if a smidge old fashioned," said Jim.

"Old fashioned? It was a ten on the schmaltz-o-meter."

"My, my, Captain Berg, are you so jaded a little act of chivalry causes you distress?"

"Oh, blow it out your ear, mister. It was in Granola Aviation's colors and had flowing ribbons hanging down saying, 'Fly Granola—we care as much as you do'."

Jim laughed aloud. "Yikes, that's a PR geek all right."

"So do I get an apology?"

"Of course. I am suitably contrite."

"The heck with contrite, I want a proper apology. An IOU for hot monkey sex might do it."

"Consider it done. I saw you on *Vogue's* social page as well as the tabloids."

"Since when do you buy *Vogue* or the tabloids?"

"Since I met you," said Jim. "It's pretty much the only way I can keep tabs on you."

"Do my antics bother you?"

"No. Like you, I knew what I bargained for when I signed on."

"Good," said Sophie. "So are we using up minutes to talk about that dirty monkey sex and agonize about why we aren't together, or are you in Mountie mode?"

"Can I have five minutes in Mountie and follow up with monkey?"

"Your time starts now—shoot."

"I'd rather not go there," said Jim.

"Right, under the circumstances, not a good word for us. Okay, as my English friends would say—*tally-ho*."

"You recently researched buying a new car, right? Wanted a Lamborghini, but settled on a Beemer?"

Sophie sighed. "Story of my life."

"You ever come across a luxury car dealership called Kickin' It Custom in Queens, New York?"

"No, should I have?"

"Dammit. It was long shot, but I need to get in there and take a look around."

"You're a cop," said Sophie, matter of factly. "Get a warrant."

"I want to get a real look, not what they want me to see. And this place only caters to the rich and famous. I need a referral from an existing customer."

"Ah-ha—I knew it all along, you're only interested in me for my connections."

"*Sophie* ... "

Sophie giggled. "Well you're fortunate because I know plenty of people with Lamborghinis. In fact, if you get *Vogue*, you saw me with Brett Larkin at the film's after party. He was bragging about taking me home in one."

"I saw him and was hoping to erase the picture from my memory. Exactly where was his hand?"

"In a cast, after I broke a finger or two. I am very particular who touches my—"

"Then I'm flattered," said Jim, smiling to himself.

"I suppose I could apologize for my brutality and ask if he knows the place."

"Would you do that for me?" asked Jim.

"I think you know the answer to that. Add the favor to my monkey IOU, and we have a deal."

"You know, I wouldn't normally want a girlfriend involved in my work," said Jim. "However, you've been shot at twice and come through it, so I'm thinking my nonsense has become routine for you."

"I wouldn't say routine. Being involved in your nonsense gives me a real buzz."

"That's not the job. That's my magnetic personality and superior sexual skills."

Sophie laughed. "Oh yeah right—I forgot about those."

"You forgot?"

"Jimmy, Jimmy, Jimmy, you are *soooo* easy." Sophie giggled.

"So when can you call Larkin?"

"After you put down the phone if you want."

"You don't have to meet him, do you?" asked Jim.

"Won't know until I call. But even if we have dinner, don't you trust me?"

Jim didn't say anything.

"Jim ... " said Sophie, in the same questioning tone he used on her.

"Sophie, look, I have to say this. When I first began looking into Granola, I thought you might be involved in the bad stuff that's going on. But as the investigation has unfolded, and I've gotten to know you, I realize you aren't. Now you've moved into a place in my life that I'm not familiar with. I can't ignore that something amazing is happening between us, because I have feelings for you I've never had before. I'm never jealous, but—"

"Maybe you simply hadn't met anyone to be jealous about?"

"That could be."

"You're not the only one in unfamiliar territory, Jim," said Sophie. "I'm surrounded by men who just want to say they've been with me, and while I may have dinner with them, it's you I want. You simply need to trust me. I'll make my enquiries, and you will get your answers. Then the day after tomorrow, I'll be in New York for three days representing Granola at the Aviation Association awards dinner. You can stay with me at the hotel and go see your dealership. Then I expect to receive payment on your IOU."

CHAPTER TWENTY-FOUR

When they left the hotel, a valet handed Jim keys to a BMW7, series Alpina.

"Nice ride," said Sophie, sliding into the passenger seat.

Jim smiled. "At one hundred-thirty-six grand it should be. The NYPD had a shit fit when I rented it, and if I so much as scuff the upholstery I'll be paying for the detailing until doomsday."

"Relax," said Sophie, hiking up her skirt. "I'll take care of things if you need a bail out. You rent the suit too?"

"Nope, that's all mine. Sister's wedding last year."

"Very sharp. If we didn't have to be somewhere, I'd rip it off you."

"You're impossible," said Jim, heading to Kickin' It Custom.

When they pulled into the showroom parking lot, a gargantuan African American minder stepped forward. Jim rolled down the window. "Sophie Berg," he said.

"Welcome," said the minder. "If you'd like to step this way, I'll park your car." He buzzed them into a showroom full of luxury automobiles.

"Ms. Berg," said the limp-handed salesman. "I'm Colton Harman. It's very nice to meet you. I saw your picture in *Vogue*, and Mr. Larkin spoke very highly of you. Would this be your driver?"

Sophie smiled. "This is my companion, Jean-Paul Therriault from Ottawa." Sophie was using an established cover for Jim. "He will be buying my vehicle, so it is he you need to convince to part with a hundred thousand dollars."

"*Ah, mais oui, Monsieur Therriault,*" said Colton. "*Comment allez-vous?*"

"*Très bien, merci,*" Jim replied. "But could we speak English, for Ms. Berg's sake?"

"Of course. My apologies, Ms. Berg. May I get you some champagne and canapés while Monsieur Therriault and I discuss business?"

"That would be very nice, and might you have a small pick-me-up available?"

Jim was surprised at Sophie's request but went along with her.

Within minutes, a waiter came from behind a screen with the champagne, canapés, and a small tray with drug sniffing accoutrements and several lines of cocaine.

Sophie demurely crossed her legs. "Okay, you two, off you go; discuss my car. I have plenty to keep me happy.

•••

Jim reappeared twenty minutes later, and noticed the lines of cocaine were gone. "Well, my dear," he said, taking Sophie's hand. "Colton and I have just about agreed on something. I will discuss it with you and call him with my answer."

When they were in the car, Jim took a deep breath. "Sophie, I know you're a singularly independent woman, but please don't tell me you snorted that coke."

Sophie laughed. "You know, I speak French fluently."

"*Sophie* ... "

"You are getting so cute with that *Sophie* whine, but please Jim, when are you going to trust me?"

"The coke?"

"Let's just get out of here."

"Are you doing this deliberately to torture me?" asked an exasperated Jim. "I tell you I care about you, and you hit me with an addiction."

Sophie giggled. "Really, are you serious? This is me, Jim. I don't even take aspirin in case it interferes with my ability to fly."

"So what did you do with it?"

Sophie removed a zip-lock bag from her purse.

"You took it. Are you insane? There are cameras all over that showroom. Somebody will have seen you."

"Doesn't matter. Whether I snorted it there, or took it home for later, they'll think I'm one of the 'in' crowd."

"Dear God, what's next?" asked Jim. "When I saw it, I about died. How did you know they would simply bring you some?"

"That buffoon Larkin told me. Apparently, this place is very well frequented for more than just its selection of cars. Did you find the lead you were looking for?"

"I think I did. I said I was shipping the car back to Ottawa for your use and wanted to ensure Kickin's shipping methods were sound. I was able to ask questions and take a peek into a couple of places not normally shown to customers. Do you know who they use for transport?"

"Granola Aviation."

Jim raised an eyebrow. "How did you—"

"Told you, I ask questions."

"They could get you dead," said Jim.

"I realize that, but I find all this cloak and dagger stuff very sexy."

"Is that why you took the cocaine—to show how dangerous and sexy you were?"

Sophie pouted. "I'm crushed; don't you know that already?"

"*Sophie* ... "

"Okay, okay, hold your horses. You said you recovered bags of cocaine from the botched run into Zeb Cove. I figured you could test what I have against it and prove the line of distribution through Kickin' It. Now, what do you want me to do next? I could go back on the roster and request the route flying the cars around ..."

Jim took Sophie's hand and kissed the knuckles. "Dear God, I've created a monster."

•••

As Jim put the car in drive, his phone rang. "Hi, Mac, what's up?" He listened for several seconds. "Oh yeah—beautiful, I'll be back tomorrow."

"You're grinning like a Cheshire cat, what gives?" asked Sophie.

"Apparently, a trooper pulled over an old guy on a suspected DUI. He attempted to resist arrest and got hauled to the station. Turns out, he's Merrill Goldwater. It appears we now have two of our smugglers."

Sophie put a hand on Jim's thigh. "Does that mean we have something else to celebrate?"

Jim grinned. "Hell, yeah!"

CHAPTER TWENTY-FIVE

When Jim entered the interrogation room, the normally calm Merrill was jumpy as corn in a kettle. "Way ya looky here," he drawled in his old mariner's voice. "'Tis da Mountie. I's been following yer nonsense fer some time. Christ, I's guessin' ya was kilt a while back."

Jim threw a couple of grainy surveillance photos of a black Dodge Ram on the table. You could just make out two men in the vehicle. While the man driving was obscured, the passenger appeared to have white-blond hair. Jim was of the opinion the men were Merrill Goldwater and Lance Deveraux. "Know anything about the shooting outside the Regent in Portland?"

"Dunno nuthin' about it," said Merrill, grinning. "Howzat fine looking uniform o' yours?"

"Or maybe the bullets were meant for Captain Berg?"

Merrill grinned. "I's just askin' about 'at nice red jacket o' yours."

"I'm sure that's what you meant," said Jim, looking towards his colleagues behind the two-way mirror. "So let's cut the small talk. I need answers. I might not be able to pin the shooting on you—yet. But I know it was you, Lance Deveraux, and Rake Jensen using the *Hesperus* to haul cocaine-filled lobster pots out of Canada."

"Ya got smokes?"

"Not the crap you suck down."

"Man, I's takin' anythin' ya got ri' now," said Merrill, swiping a hand across his mouth. "Them wet behin' the ears hick chicken-shit bible tumpers behind 'at glass dunno real life fra a hole in head. Got jack in the way of pacifiers. Even offers me instant coffee—wha's tha' slop made of anyway—gnat's pee?" Turning to the uniformed cop at the door, he spat. "Ya gonna te' me 'ow my boy is?"

"Your boy?"

"Lance. He my gran'son, kin, so law sez ya gotta tell me bout 'im."

"No," said Jim.

"Den I don't gotta tell ya shit eeder."

"Okay by me. I've got smokes, decent coffee, and all my relatives are healthy." Jim turned to leave.

"Okay, okay," said Merrill. "Gimme a smoke."

Jim placed cigarettes and a book of matches on the table, and Merrill's sinewy hand clawed open the packet and lit up. Sucking the narcotic deep into his lungs, he quickly recovered his *chutzpah*, and rasped at the uniformed officer. "May yaself useful, pig—ge' me a decen' cup o' joe."

The uniform looked at Jim who nodded.

"An' a Danish!"

Jim nodded again, and the officer left.

Merrill sucked nicotine in deep. "Beat cops—damn-blasted sap-sucking morons."

Jim lowered his voice and leaned forward. "Lance is okay— flesh wound, broken ankle. He's refusing to help us, and knows you're here."

"Good," said Merrill dragging on the cigarette. While he was relieved his lover was not badly injured, Merrill knew it was Lance who'd taken the shots at Jim and the pilot. The old man knew the penalty for smuggling cocaine would pretty much determine where he'd spend the rest of his life. However, he intended to do everything he could to mitigate Lance's sentence.

"Now I've given you something, let's hear what you've got."

"I wanna speak to 'im," demanded Merrill.

Jim smiled. "You know better than that."

"Wha' if we trade? I'll tell ya what I knows for a few words."

"Maybe later."

Merrill sized up Jim and took a final drag on his cigarette. When ash fell in a powdery column on the interrogation table, he brushed it on the floor and crushed the filter underfoot. "'E say anything 'bout our little cruise?"

"I think you know the answer to that."

"Tougher 'an he looks, ain't he?" Merrill lit up another cigarette. "Waddaya wanna know?"

"Where's the rest of the cocaine?"

"Away."

"Where?" asked Jim.

"Come on, Sergeant, 'you know better than that.'" He mimicked Jim exactly.

Jim smiled. "Cute, but unnecessary. We know Jensen hauled some hold-alls to Orient Heights and handed it to—shall we say, a snappy dressing dude who gets ferried around in a Beemer 760Li out of Kickin' It Custom in Queens, New York."

A slight coloring in Merrill's cheeks let Jim know he was on the mark.

"So wha' more ya want from me?"

"Nothing regarding that, thanks," said Jim. "Where's Rake Jensen?"

"Scum suckin' fly-blow shou be at da bottom of a goddamn lake."

"I take it you had a falling out."

Merrill sucked heavily on his smoke, blowing an angry cloud to the ceiling. "Where's da goddamn Joe?" Merrill paused at the precise moment the officer came in with Starbucks coffee and his favorite Danish. "Damn, lookie 'ere. Blue boy got it zactly right. Gotta try askin' fur sumthin' else." He reduced the second cigarette to a precarious column of ash and trod the butt underfoot. "Ya see, tha's why I dun smoke this crap. It got no body, no juice—gimme a stogie anytime. Now, they's got balls—chewable heaven man, ya know wha' I mean?"

"Cut the review," said Jim. "And answer the question."

Firing up a third cigarette, Merrill took a drag and parked it on the edge of the table. Then he took a large swig of coffee and a bite of Danish. "Shit, da real stuff. I's honored."

"Delighted we could accommodate. Where's Jensen?"

"Dunno, but if'n I gits me 'ands on him, he'll wish he ne'er crossed me."

"So if he crossed you, you owe him nothing," said Jim. "Help us find him."

"Ain't the way I work, man. 'Sides, wha' difference anythin' make? The snow dun melted in the city by now. Ya ain't gettin' nothin' bu' crap shit from Rake Jensen."

"What about the crystal he's hawking?" asked Jim.

Merrill let out a derogatory grunt. "Kin only sell 'at crap to out-of-towners lookin' to jazz up a weekend. Quality ain't wuth a damn. Ya ain't gonna make nuthin' outta dat."

"We're told you supplied him with the fixings," added Jim.

"Prove it." Confident in his ability to hide his past dealings, Merrill casually blew a smoke ring into the air.

Cromwell held up a set of keys.

"Wha' ya gut der?" Merrill asked, masking surprise.

Jim smiled as he placed the keys on the table. "The desk sergeant, you know, one of those wet behind the ears chicken-shit bible thumpers who don't know real life from a hole in head, he noticed that keys taken from you and Lance looked identical. So we isolated a particular pair that looked like house keys and because they are specialized security keys, we contacted the maker."

"Wha' ya mean? Does I look li' a man wi' a 'ouse needin' security keys?"

"Right now I'm not exactly sure what you look like, Merrill. But I do know where you and Lance live."

The smoke rings disintegrated, but Merrill's edge did not. "So wha' ya lookin' fur, a *ménage-à-trois* or sumthin'? Ya froggies fro' Canada like a bit o' variety, I's told."

Jim pulled a piece of paper from his pocket. "When we go to 3B White Whale Wharf, Frenchman's Bay, I'm sure we'll find enough evidence to put you away for the rest of your natural life. Lance probably won't do any better."

"Goin' an' findin' is two differen' tings. 'Sides, I's been 'ere afor an' I got big frens wi' giant frens. Ya ain't gonna pin nuthin' on nobody."

Jim paced. "So let's get this straight for the record. You were okay letting Jensen drive off, knowing Lance was shot and bleeding on the jetty. By all accounts, he didn't turn back to see if either of you was dead or alive. Neither did he take a minute to make sure you, the old guy, made it to a truck. Then, when you got to Orient Heights to hand over the goods, he double-crossed you, and you got zip. Thought of no one but himself. Not you. And certainly not Lance." Cromwell waited for some sort of reaction from Merrill. Merrill didn't give him one. "It's quite amusing, really. After all these years, the infamously slick Dante Goldwater Merrill got screwed over by a better man. And it turns out that man is one of them hicks from the backwoods. That feel good at all? You're losing your edge, old man. Seems you can't handle the pressure anymore." Merrill said nothing. "A small time meth dealer took money from you. It's probably happened before, but you were sharp and on the ball. You got even. This time, not so much. But Lance? Now he's different. He's your other half, and that bastard Rake just left him stone cold, bleeding and busted. Your boy could have died right there on the dock. Could have bled out, his life seeping away while Jensen was sitting home drinking beer and spending your money. You really okay with that?"

Merrill delicately picked a couple of non-existent grounds from the end of his tongue. He took his time considering the ramifications of what he was about to say and how he was to say it. "Well aren't you a slicky-dicky, Mister Mountie." Merrill had lost his mariner accent, but not his sarcastic edge. "You make a compelling argument when you plead to my softer side." His eyes glazed over at the thought of Lance hurt and bleeding. "Still, love me or hate me, there's no getting away from it. I had a good run and have no regrets. But you're right. My Lance is entirely different. With understanding and a break or two, he has the potential to be somebody."

"Well," said a surprised Cromwell. "It seems confession is good for something more than the soul. The accent was fun but let's hope it's not the only thing you drop today."

"Before we go on," said Merrill. "Let's drop one thing right here and now. I still have friends, and I promise Jensen is going to pay for hurting Lance. I think you're good, in your own way, but my guys will deal with him long before you find him."

"So was it you or your 'guys' who attempted to deal with me outside the Regent?"

Merrill smiled. "Self-preservation is a powerful force."

Jim looked at the two-way glass. "You just admitted to attempted murder."

"Is that right," said Merrill, stubbing out his cigarette and lighting another.

"Is that your way of asking for a deal here?"

Merrill smiled and pushed his empty cup towards Jim. "Got any more coffee?"

"You can have a pot if you deliver me Rake Jensen."

"As I said, suffering is the way I want that shit to go. However, I'll give you a little consolation prize."

"Oh yeah?" said Jim.

"I'm guessing if you want to shut down his operation, you might have a word or two with his wife. She works at the Well Head in Limerick."

"She shouldn't be working in a bar at sixteen."

"Tell it to the Marines."

Jim smiled. "You know where they live?"

"Make it my place to vet employees in case I need some leverage. Last time I checked, the two of them were holed up in a beat-up trailer somewhere in the woods back of Victoria Falls. Logging trail E407 will get you started, but you're not going to find the campsite trail unless you know it. So from where I sit, the only way to get where you want to be is through her." Merrill lit another cigarette and took a long drag. It was as if he knew it would be his last for a while. "That's all you're getting until I talk to Lancelot."

"Lancelot?" asked Jim.

"Lance Deveraux."

Jim raised an eyebrow. "I'll ask the officer to put you in the cell next to him. That good enough?"

Merrill lit another cigarette. "Do I have a choice?"

CHAPTER TWENTY-SIX

When Jim finally got hold of Sophie, she had just arrived at her hotel in Baltimore. "Everything okay?" he asked. "Your phone was on 'do not disturb' again, but the override code didn't work. What's that all about?"

"I'm not sure," said Sophie. "I'd heard odd noises on the line, and as it's a Granola phone, I had IT run a diagnostic. They said it was probably sun spots or some such nonsense."

"My phone wasn't having problems. Wouldn't sun spots affect all phones?"

"God knows. I'm a pilot, not a techno-geek," Sophie replied. "But it doesn't matter now. You got me, and that's the important thing."

Jim frowned. Protecting himself and looking for things out of the normal routine were second nature. It was troubling to think he may have dragged Sophie more deeply into his world. "Has anything else unusual happened since you left Maine?" asked Jim.

"Not that I've noticed. What are you getting at?"

Jim smiled. "Don't miss much, do you?"

"All part of my charm."

"Have you had any feelings that you're being followed or watched? Is your mail being delivered as usual?"

"Good grief, as far as I know—who monitors that?"

"You should, Sophie."

"You're freaking me out now," she said. "Since when does an ordinary American have to monitor their mail?"

"Since you tied up with me."

Sophie took a deep breath. "So what are you suggesting?"

"I may have dropped the ball where you are concerned," said Jim. "I think someone might be listening in on our conversations."

"Why?"

"They know about us."

"Not from me they don't."

"If Granola's grapevine is anything like the police department, they don't need you to say anything—they know anyway," said Jim. "Do you have phone card?"

"Sure. The company still sends me to God forsaken places without cell service. I'm prepared for all eventualities."

"Do me a favor. Go find a public phone and call me."

Five minutes later, Jim's phone rang.

"Where are you now?" he asked.

"In the hotel lobby." Sophie giggled. "It was momentarily worrying, but truthfully, this is so awesome. I feel like *Mata Hari*. Do I get a pair of shoes that turn into a bomb?"

"*Sophie … *"

"Sorry, defense mechanism. I know—this is serious. What's up?"

"I wanted to let you know the case is taking me up country for a few days. I may not be back when you arrive in Portland."

"Can I still go to the cabin?"

"If you want to. Will you be all right 'til I get there?"

"Sure. I have your spare key. I presume you have food and booze, and I know where you keep the gun and ammo. Plus Tommy Ray Farnsworth at the post office will be happy to keep me company should I get cold at night."

"Tommy Ray is barely sixteen," said Jim. "Do I need to arrest you?"

"Not at the moment. However, if you don't get back to me by Friday, hot, sweaty and in need of a rub down, you can slap on the cuffs."

Jim laughed aloud. "You'd like that, wouldn't you?"

"Hold onto that thought, Mr. Mountie, 'cos I'm always looking to add to my repertoire."

"You mean you have tricks I haven't seen?"

"You better believe it," said Sophie. "So what's up country?"

"Apparently, the guys we have in custody are a couple. They live in a place on the waterfront in Frenchman's Bay. I'm going up to search the residence and see if I can find any leads on who's handing them the drugs in Canada. We know the Pakistani end, we now know the New York piece … it's this bit in the middle that's sketchy."

"Will it be dangerous?" asked Sophie.

"Do you think that would make a difference to my line of inquiry?"

"You're a single-minded nutcase, so probably not."

"Then don't think about it. Just trust in the fact that a higher power is in control," said Jim. "In the meantime, we're going to continue with the telephone cloak and dagger stuff because I don't trust Granola. The last thing I want is anyone there hearing our conversations."

"You're being a bit melodramatic, aren't you?"

"Your phone override is on the fritz and there are weird noises on your phone. You've been shot at twice, and while I think I know who did that, until I'm sure, we'll assume the shooter is still on the loose. Do the math."

"Technically, we know who shot at me the second time."

"Sophie, don't be flippant. I'm not taking any chances."

"So how do I talk to you from now on?"

"You really do miss me, don't you," said Jim.

"I'm not answering that on the grounds it may incriminate me," said Sophie. "I simply know the phone interception fairies will be able to pinpoint your location if I called your phone. We certainly don't want that. Besides, what if I need to relay some information about the cabin?"

Jim laughed. "Quit back-peddling. You're worried about me. How sweet. You really care and you're too chicken-shit to come right out and tell me."

"Okay, I admit it. You are sort of addictive."

"So now I know you're *totally* besotted, I'll have more incentive to hurry back to the cabin."

"Who said anything remotely resembling *totally* besotted? I recall a minor hint about a possibly temporary condition."

"Liar, liar, pants on fire."

"Stop with the cutesy talk. Okay, I do need to talk to you now and again. How do we connect?"

"Good point about the tracking. Call me on Mac's phone, 555-8690, until I arrange something untrackable."

"Get enough minutes for nights of phone sex."

"You are the most—"

"Important thing, other than work, in your life. I know, that's why you love me."

"Excuse me?" asked Jim.

"Bye-bye, Mr. Mountie. I'm getting some shut-eye now. But just remember our Alexander Pope connection when you question your feelings for me. What did he say: '*No, fly me, fly me, far as pole from pole; rise Alps between us and whole oceans roll! Ah, come not, write not, think not once of me, nor share one pang of all I felt for thee.*'"

"Very cute, but I'm not sure I want you to equate me with Abelard," said Jim. "Wasn't he castrated for loving Eloise?"

Sophie laughed. "Best I could come up with on short notice."

"The more I know you, the more fascinating you become," whispered Jim. "For an analytical pilot you're pretty sensitive."

"Is that good or bad?"

"Delightfully unexpected."

"Good, I'm glad I can surprise you. But remember, Jim, life is full of surprises. Despite the fact you're a top-notch investigator, I hope you realize you should never judge a book by its cover. Be careful out there, Jim."

"I'm always careful. See you soon." Jim smiled as he hung up the phone.

CHAPTER TWENTY-SEVEN

When Cromwell tied up with the local police in Frenchman's Bay, he was surprised they led him to a fishing tackle shack on the waterfront. The dilapidated lean-to might have been the sort of place the old mariner Merrill would live, but now that Jim knew him to be considerably more refined than he first appeared, he expected something more up-market. Nevertheless, armed with a search warrant and the keys taken as evidence, he opened the weathered plank door and went into the shack's dark and cramped confines.

Jim's lone flashlight illuminated the interior's shabby appointments, for grime and webs had long since rendered the windows impervious to light. And as he stepped forward, the air hung thick with the dank smell of dead fish and corruption. An accompanying officer propped open the shack's door and cranked the ancient casements, but it did little to lighten the space abused and lifeless from the wear and tear of countless fishing seasons. Cromwell reached for the light pull of a naked bulb hanging beneath the buckled board ceiling. Far from helping to facilitate the search, its meager illumination made the dwelling's deterioration more obvious and the depths of its fetid corners more contagious.

Within minutes, officers had removed the room's decrepit furniture to the wharf. With the room devoid of the personality its shabby possessions bestowed, Jim was left center-floor, speculating on the mysteries of a ten-by-ten wooden box. Tapping walls and floors, he made a systematic sweep of the shack and opened an inordinately large coat closet containing a bulky assortment of fishermen's garb. The kitchen area's cupboards revealed the obvious: condensed milk, coffee, cube sugar, and an ancient tin of cookies. A coffeepot, grounds thick and gritty about its base, cracked cups, dusty and immovable, and glasses etched dull from years of use completed the picture. But far from discovering clues pointing towards Merrill's trade, Jim's findings were limited to mice droppings and the shriveled corpses of long dead arachnids. As he absorbed every sordid nuance of the space, his neck hair bristled, his gut screamed conspiracy, and Sophie's parting words bit deep into his psyche. *Never judge a book by its cover.*

As he slowly turned, panning his flashlight up and down, Jim remembered Merrill saying, "Going and finding are two different things." That was certainly true, and Jim did little more than breathe shallowly, letting the specter of the old man—the old furniture, the old room, and the flickering old bulb—wash over him. He had no doubt everything he wanted was right in front of him. It was simply hidden, just as the real Merrill was hidden, in plain sight. A thought niggled at him. If Merrill actually lived in this shack, why were the products in the cupboards so old? The brands stored were well known; however, the labels of some of them had long since changed. The coffeepot, while perfectly appropriate for the old potbelly stove in the corner, hadn't seen use this side of prohibition. And the condiments, now sold in soulless plastic cylinders, were displayed in metal-capped bottles, outlawed decades ago. Merrill might look like a beaten down slob, but Jim knew a man with Merrill's reputation as a successful criminal would not live in such squalor.

Jim quietly stood, focused his mind, and enveloped himself in the essence of the room. But the space taunted him and was as deceitful and incongruous as the owner. Something wasn't right. He was missing the point of the shack.

And then it dawned on him. Merrill was like a hunter covering his hiding place with foliage to try to fool his prey. This shack was his *hide*. Except the inside was the disguise. The wily old man had created this illusion to put off anyone who ventured inside. Jim simply had to come at it again, inside out.

Beginning at the front door, Jim systematically worked his way around the room's perimeter. However, the dull thuds emitted from his stamping bore no distinct difference from one area of floor to another. Tapping walls again, he strained his ears for the minutest echo from within. The salt-dried timbers mocked his insensitivity and gave up nothing. Then he stood with his face to the front door. Closing his eyes, he pictured the room as he first encountered it. He wasn't trying to remember what was missing. He was attempting to capture what was always there. Counting slowly to five, Jim turned and opened his eyes. And in the millisecond before his eyes adjusted, like a child full of expectation upon encountering a magician's box, he saw it. A bi-textural, almost invisible smoothness around the area in front of the closet. The wood was a little shinier there. Its color a shade deeper. And as he stepped forward, kneeling in place, he felt the shallowness of wear beneath his fingertips.

Looking with focused eyes, he saw that where he stood appeared no different from the rest of the grubby floor. However, the spot on which he'd stopped was alive with kinetic energy. Stooping low, he rapped on the boards. Then he tapped a yard to either side. The floor there was denser, the boards rougher, and the nail heads sharp, defined, and unworn. Merrill might think he had accounted for everything, but Jim knew differently. No matter how careful, no matter how clever, the bad guys were, more often than not, they lost. Jim never underestimated his foes, and was never surprised at the lengths they went to cover their tracks. But he knew the criminal mind had an inherent flaw. It always believed it was smarter than anyone else. It was that pride that usually came before the fall. Jim smiled. His intellect had brought him this far. His instinct would lead him on.

Slowly rising, Jim glanced around. There was considerable threshold wear at the front door—access and egress made that normal. There was very little below the cupboards or in front of the sink, where he'd expect it to be. However, the highest traffic area seemed to be in front of the closet, which prompted a thought to cross Jim's mind. In such a diminutive habitat, why waste space on such a large coat closet?

Re-opening the closet's flimsy crackled paint doors, Jim studied the garments hanging within. They appeared entirely appropriate for fishermen, but something about the slickers didn't jive. They appeared used, but were un-scuffed, with no tears or gashes—like they hadn't actually been worked in. He rubbed the fabric between his thumb and forefinger—it was grainy and distressed. However, when he brought the garments to his nose, they smelled—soapy. It was as if the slickers had been aged by the hot cycle of a washing machine.

Slipping one of the slickers over his muscular six-foot frame, Jim discovered it was several sizes too small. Moreover, when he invited several officers back into the shack, and they, in turn, tried on a slicker, none fit—save one. Because slickers are traditionally roomy to enable the wearer to work freely, the only person who fit comfortably in any of the assembled gear was Officer Paula James. A five-foot-two bundle of energy, she weighed no more than a hundred pounds soaking wet. Jim smiled; even the diminutive Lance would have trouble working in such gear.

Pressing on, Jim lay the garments aside and shined his flashlight into the closet. And there, in the darkest corner, sat another anomaly. He unclipped the Swiss Army knife always on his belt and poked at the treasure. Dragging it fully into his light, he recognized it as a piece of toast. Probably whole wheat, teeth marks visible. His head inclined. What was a piece of toast doing in the closet? It couldn't have been there long because one of the multiple species of rodents inhabiting the waterfront would have snapped it up. But here it was, untouched and relatively fresh. He sheathed his knife and bagged the evidence to take saliva samples for DNA comparison.

Jim was now in the closet facing out, and instinct had him running his fingers around the door jam. Deftly feeling its woody imperfections, he stopped on the smooth chill of a piece of metal, two fingers wide and two across. He applied pressure to the plate, and a faint hissing preceded a give behind him. He turned, and as his body pressed on the back of the closet, the wall gave way.

Smiling, Jim cautiously stepped into a crypt-like vestibule. Like those in a cellar, steps led up to another door. Urging the officers to follow through the back of the closet, Jim drew his gun and proceeded up the stairs. He found the door unlocked and pushed it open. A flash of brilliance blinded him, and he dropped to the floor and rolled aside.

With no idea what he'd encountered, Jim remained floored for several seconds. As his eyes adjusted, he became aware that the brightness was merely the sun, streaming through the expansive windows of the room in which he was crouching. As he shouted a warning to the officers following, and waited for them to emerge from the darkness, he went to the window. He was looking down a hill, and there at the bottom was the shack he'd originally entered. Jim smiled. It was a perfect hide. From outside there appeared to be no connection between the two structures. But in climbing through the shack's closet and ascending the cellar stairs, he had gone from the water's edge to the house on the hill above.

When Jim's team had assembled, they proceeded through the house with guns drawn. Jim made a cursory sweep of the first floor. From the anteroom, through large living and dining rooms, and a sumptuously decorated sitting room, he paused in the gourmet kitchen. Whatever Mr. Merrill Goldwater had been doing, it appeared he had been very successful at it. From the kitchen, he circled back to the living room, full of expensive furniture, sumptuous fabrics and a wealth of *objets d'art*. Jim shook his head. Using his persona as a local fisherman, down and almost out, Merrill had entirely fooled the authorities about his true personality and lifestyle. However, now that he had found the lion's den, Jim was confident all his questions would be answered.

After determining that the house was empty, the entire team assembled back in the living room. Jim allocated rooms and told each officer to proceed with an in-depth search of their allotted area. He was curious about the only locked door in the space and elected to concentrate on the living room.

After trying every key on Merrill's ring, none fit. So Jim removed the hinge pins and wrestled the solid oak door aside. He uncovered an inner metal door secured by a sophisticated locking mechanism with a tumbler. A pop key fit perfectly, but Jim knew it was useless without the combination. Having progressed from gnawing questions, through excited anticipation, to this moment of frustration, Jim kicked at the taunting steel. However, he knew without doubt that whatever lay behind the door, would more than make up for his months of frustration working on the case.

Pacing across the living room, Jim knew the only people who could get the door open were the owner, which was unlikely, the manufacturer, which would be time consuming since he would have to get and act upon a warrant, or one of a special group of ex-felons who occasionally worked for the police department. He flipped his cell and within minutes, one such person was in a helicopter and on his way from Boston to Frenchman's Bay.

•••

By late afternoon, the steel door was open, revealing an impressive vault. Forensics dusted and cataloged the contents, finding a large amount of cash, gold bullion, and several kinds of drugs—none of which would be as damaging to Merrill as the meticulously detailed, leather-bound journals, dated 1995–2004.

As Jim flipped through the pages of the most recent volume, it was evident Merrill was an exceptional record-keeper. Years of smuggling missions and sales of all manner of illicit commodities were documented on the pages. The wily old mariner had amassed a fortune, and his client list read like a *who's who* of the underworld's elite. But the most telling names for Jim were not the criminal element, New England's *nouveau riche*, or one of dozens of "regular Joes" partaking of Merrill's goods. Jim was more interested in the companies involved in more recent happenings. Kickin' It Custom had contracted Merrill, as the head of the Albatross Alliance, to salvage and deliver a consignment of cocaine from local lobster pots. Golden Lance Historical, also owned by Merrill, distributed narcotics all over the country under the guise of delivering fabrics and rugs of historical importance to museums and galleries. And most disturbingly, Dante Goldwater Merrill was a major shareholder in Granola Aviation, confirming Jim's suspicion that the airline was a cover for more than one criminal level.

It was now imperative he talk to Sophie.

CHAPTER TWENTY-EIGHT

The sun was coming up when Rake woke, and with his head pounding fit to burst, he hadn't a clue where he was. His truck appeared to be on an angle, and when he tried to move, he found he was wedged in the space beneath the steering wheel. It felt like someone was standing on his back, and, immediately sober, Rake knew he'd driven off the road. He had no feeling in the leg beneath him as he wriggled into a bracing position. Pushing as hard as he dare on the free leg sticking out behind him, he peered over the dash. His vehicle was tight against a large pine. Cursing aloud, he realized there was but one way to extricate himself.

Opening the driver's side door, Rake held firm to the truck sill, locked his free leg against the passenger door, and pushed. It took considerable effort, but like a carcass off a meat hook, his dead weight flopped into a water-filled ditch.

Rake could do nothing but wait for his circulation to return, and after several minutes of rubbing, he was finally able to stand and stamp life into his pinned leg. Then he clambered from the ditch and surveyed the vehicle for damage. He'd run across a verge, down a slope, and was straddling a brook alongside a stand of pines. A large tree had stopped his forward motion, and while he could see the Ford had sustained some front-end damage, he had no idea what being in such a precarious position had done to the engine.

Being a sometime logger, Rake was an expert at getting trucks and equipment out of ditches and potholes. So dragging a come-along from his tool chest, he looped it around another tree and inched the vehicle from its resting place.

After an hour of cranking, the Ford was in a position where Rake could try the engine. It spluttered to life, allowing him to reverse the truck up the remainder of the slope. However, as he started down the trail, whining noises indicated the engine had sustained damage. As long as he made it back to his trailer, he could jack up the vehicle and make the needed repairs.

As dawn gave way to better light, Rake looked around. He knew exactly where he was —

halfway between his place and Woody's. And figuring the old pick-up would last long enough for him to get to the mercantile, he decided to pick up his munitions.

• • •

Woody was all smiles when Rake appeared at his back door. "Hey, amigo, how's it hangin'; yer get paid?"

"Not so's ya'd notice. That sack o' shit Merrill tried ta hose me."

"Told yer he's a tricky bastard, but yer got cash enough? 'Cos I can't hold onto the merchandise; it's hotter 'an a hooker's pussy."

"Ya, I got it covered, ten thousand, right?"

"Nice work, my man. How's 'bout we celebrate wi' a cup o' Woody's best mountain brew?"

"I'd rather have a Bud."

"Ah, yer got no spirit of adventure."

"Sure I do. Be sellin' this lot up top an' spirit o' adventure be more 'an double what I paid ya here."

"Yer can try, but those guys don't welcome outsiders."

"Ain't no outsider," said Rake. "Got a cousin connected."

"Yer mean yer wife has a cousin connected. Ya not taking her up country in her state?"

"Hadn't planned to. Got her pass, though," said Rake.

"Then yer ok. How yer gettin' up there?"

"Back roads most, don't wanna attrack attention."

"Think yer already did. That old Ford a yorn needs some serious TLC."

Rake swiped an eyebrow. "Ran into a ditch a ways back. I can fix it."

"I also hear there's a local helping catalog the trails. Yer see anyone around?"

"Nah, though I's boosting a buck a while back, un the old lady near blew some chick's head off."

"She frum away?"

"Look like it. All dandified fer a woodland stroll."

"Yer better quit giving that little gal a gun; she'll have the feds rainin' down on yer."

"Ah, jack 'em, they's all a bunch o' crap heads. Couldna get me out o' Zeb Cove; sure ain't gettin' me in my own backyard."

"Watch yerself is all," said Woody. "Yer taking yer chemistry stash?"

"Don't have much left."

"I'd ditch it; I hear them feds is out to bust the crystal camps anyway. Ain't worth a damn compared to selling munitions."

"Good t' know. Don't worry about me. I got a plan."

"Okay, so nice do'in bizniss wi' yer." Woody opened the connecting door to the mercantile. "Hey, Billy Jo," he yelled. "Move yer lazy pussy and come help a customer." Woody fist bumped Rake. "See yer 'round."

"Doubt it," said Rake. "Thanks for the heads-up."

• • •

There was no sign of life when Rake arrived at his campsite, and that suited him fine. As he sat in the truck and counted the remainder of his money, he was left with eight thousand six hundred and fifty dollars. Peeling off the odd six-fifty for gas and supplies to trade, he shoved the remainder in a paper bag. Then he placed it with the guns, ammunition, explosives, and incendiaries in a bunker hidden under his woodpile.

Relief washed over Rake as he sat in his trailer. However, after he'd downed a couple of Buds, the consequences of the botched job and his wrecked truck sank in. Nobody but his wife had any idea where he was located in the backwoods, so he felt confident in lying low there before venturing out to get supplies and heading north. Nevertheless, he'd made a powerful enemy in Merrill, and any number of crack heads, desperate for a baggie of something special, would report his whereabouts to the old man.

Spitting expletives, Rake lobbed his empty beer can into the sink, staggered to the trailer's squalid bedroom, and pushing aside his sleeping wife, crashed into a drunken sleep.

• • •

It was eleven A.M. when Rake woke. He couldn't remember sleeping so soundly, but as he stretched, twinges in his back reminded him he'd spent several hours wedged under the steering wheel of his truck. Calling out for Cele to bring the Bengay, he got no answer. It was clear she'd gone out, and guessing why, he checked his back pocket. Without waking him, she'd removed two hundred dollars. In the past, such action would warrant him beating the crap out of her; today he'd let it pass. She'd soon be out of his life.

The grinding whine of his of Ford's engine galvanized him into action. He went out to the trailer's stoop and found his wife reaching into the truck bed for groceries.

"Waddaya do with my money, ya thieving bitch?"

"Hi, Rake," said Cele nervously. "The truck's making weird noises. I think you should look at it."

"I know that, ya thick bitch. Why ya think I had money in my pocket? But you just had to go into town spending. Now the whole world knows we don't got no reliable transportation."

"Christ, don't have a cow. I went to Woody's, and for your information, he already knew. What ya been cookin' up with him anyway?"

"None of your friggin' bizniss." Rake dragged two cases of beer from the truck bed. "Now where the hell we get money for parts?"

"Since when that bother you? Go down the coast and boost a car off one of them out-of-towners. They won't care; they's got insurance and all."

"And how we get there, wiseass?" asked Rake, popping a Bud. "You're lucky you made it to Woody's and back."

"So go local. I hear tell the guy moved into the Neverson cabin got a fine looking vehicle. He's from across the border, so ya know he got money to burn, and look here … " Cele flipped open an *Entertainment Weekly*.

"Why ya wastin' money on that crap?"

"Look at her." Cele pointed to a picture of a woman in a dress. "Ain't that the blonde I shot at? Woody say she some sort of pilot and flies around all them Hollywood celebrities."

"How the hell Woody know that?"

Cele shrugged. "How he know anythin'? He just does. Don't matter. Gotta be two vehicles right there at the cabin. Let's go get us one."

CHAPTER TWENTY-NINE

Sophie had her headphones on and was fully engaged in a track off the new Daughtry album before she noticed the truck in the drive. It was considerably more beaten up than when she'd last seen it. And its driver, still heavily pregnant, was waddling towards her armed again with a shotgun. Sophie lay down the pool vacuum and made her way to her chaise where she had her phone on a side table. However, before she could reach for it, her visitor fired a round into the pool. Sophie took a deep breath and imagined she was in her aircraft dealing with an emergency. This wasn't the time for nerves. "What do you want?" she demanded, moving towards the chaise.

"You stay right there and stand still," said Cele. "Nothin's gonna happen if you give us the keys to your vehicle."

"Keys? If I'm standing still how can I give you anything?" said Sophie, locking her eyes with the teenager.

"If they's in the house, go get 'em."

Sophie's leg hit the chaise. She sat abruptly, and in doing so hit Jim's emergency number on the speed dial. The phone beeped out its dialing cadence.

"What you just do?" said the teen, moving towards Sophie as fast as her bulk would allow. "Go get 'em right now, ma'am," said the teenager in a small, nervous voice. "And I won't have to use the other barrel."

"As I recall you aren't very good with that thing."

The teenager blushed. "You took me by surprise is all. This time I got yer dead to rights."

"Cele!" yelled a male voice from the woods. "Quit whining; it don't make no never mind," said Rake. "Hey, Blondie, I ain't afraid to blow ya away—go get the fuckin' keys."

At that moment, Sophie's cell rang. It was Jim returning her call. "That's probably the hardware store," said Sophie casually. "They have an urgent delivery for me. If I don't answer, they'll simply call my boyfriend who lives here. I'd sure like you to meet him."

"Word is he's a Mountie. That right?" asked Rake.

Sophie smiled.

"And I hear you're his fancy piece from out the magazines."

"I wouldn't exactly say that," said Sophie.

"Answer it," said Rake. "One wrong word an' I'll blow yer head off."

Sophie hit speak. "Hi, Eileen, yeah, thought it might be you. I'm just cleaning leaves out of the pool."

"Eileen?" asked Jim. "Sophie, it's me, you must have ESP. I was just about to call you."

"Yeah, yeah, no problem. Did my gardening equipment from *Rateau's* arrive?" Sophie deliberately emphasized the French word for rake. "They promised I'd have both items today."

"Gardening equipment … *rateau*?" asked Jim. "Is somebody there, Sophie? Jesus, is Rake Jensen there?"

"Yeah, that's both of them—the big round bucket and the weed whacker thing. Looks like I'm not going to have to put up with the backwoods overgrowth much longer. Any chance Mac could swing by with the equipment?"

"Stall as long as you can, Sophie," said Jim. "I'm an hour out of Frenchmen's Bay, but somebody will get there."

"Okay good, this afternoon." Sophie hung up the phone.

"Now why did ya go do that?" asked Rake.

"I don't know what you mean."

"Goddam women. Ya'll think yer so smart. Leroy Kelly been Eileen's guy since high school. *Mac* is the state's local pig. He's a useless sack o' shit—couldn't find blood in a knackers' yard. An' fer sure he don't deliver no equipment lest it be attached to his cruiser. An' I also know that it's not forty-five minutes since he's headin' t' Newfield. Ya screwed, Blondie, he's way on the wrong side o' helpin' ya. Move it an' get those goddam keys. Cele, get yer fat ass t' the truck. Anybody come up that drive, blast 'em."

Sophie took a step towards the walkout basement where the gun was kept.

"Stand still." Rake fired a shot into the ground in front of Sophie. "Gimme yer phone." When Sophie handed it over, he lobbed it into the pool. "No more interruptions."

Sophie turned and looked directly at Rake. "What are you going to do with me?"

"All us want is yer car, lady."

"How do I know you won't take the keys and shoot me?"

"Yer don't. Move," snapped Rake.

"I don't have a car," said Sophie.

Rake hesitated a minute, trying to process what she'd said. "Yer can't out here wi'out a car. Stop wastin' time, and get the fuckin' keys."

"I don't live here. I'm just visiting," said Sophie. "My boyfriend has the car."

"Yer full o' shit."

"So, go look in the garage."

"Git goin'," said Rake, motioning with his shotgun. When they arrived at the garage, Rake looked through the window. "Fuck it, ain't that a bitch."

"What's goin' on, Rake?" yelled Cele from beside the truck.

"Shut up an' let me think. Okay, Blondie, ya seen us up close, an' know we got a piece o' crap truck. I got no choice; you be dead."

Sophie's heart skipped a beat as she looked into the cold, dead-fish eyes of the man in front of her. She knew the property well enough to realize she couldn't make a run for anywhere. She elected to bargain. However, before she could say anything, Cele was in front of her.

"Yer not killin' her," snapped the youngster, standing between Sophie and Rake.

Rake pointed his gun at Cele. "Since when yer give me orders?"

"I'm not, but look at it this way," pleaded Cele. "So far, you ain't never killed nobody. Cops'll fry yer if ya do. And she be famous, gotta be worth sumthin' to somebody. We kin trade her for a boat load of money."

"Easier ta shoot her."

"No, no, let's take her to the trailer. I'll watch over her real good, and when she comes up missing on TV, we'll know who to ask for money. Besides, if the baby comes, I'm gonna need some help."

Rake swiped a hand across his forehead. "Don' give a rat's ass about that, but a ransom might work. You, Blondie, in the truck." He motioned with his gun.

Cele opened the truck door. "We can't all fit in here. Look at her, she's a giraffe."

"Yer can sit in back wi' the gun on her," said Rake.

"Are you crazy?" screamed Cele. "One jolt and I'm birthing this baby."

"Jesus, Mary, and Joseph, quit whining." With that, he swung his gun and the stock hit Sophie in the face. Blood gushed from her nose as she slumped to the floor.

CHAPTER THIRTY

As Jim pulled onto the cabin's drive, he could see two state trooper cruisers parked. If he'd been in the city, there might have been more, along with local police, SWAT, and all manner of uniforms. But in rural Maine, barring a militia skirmish, two troopers were as intense as it got. Mac was waiting as Jim pulled to a halt.

"It was all quiet when we got here, Jim. I'm really sorry, but Sophie is nowhere to be found."

Jim's jaw tightened and his fists clenched. "Do you think Jensen took her?"

Mac shrugged. "After all that's happened to the two of you, and what you discovered in Frenchmen's, are you sure it was Jensen?"

"Absolutely," said Jim. "Sophie used the word, *rateau*. It's French for 'rake,' and she mentioned a large round bucket. I'm assuming that was a reference to the very pregnant Mrs. Jensen."

"Wow, she's not only a cool customer, she's one smart cookie."

"She's a pilot; being cool under pressure goes with the territory, but she's not smart enough to steer clear of me."

Mac smiled. "It's that fatal Mountie charm of yours. I'm sure she'll be all right, Jim. Jensen's not a killer."

"That we know of. I called Mark Neverson. He's been working on re-mapping the logging trails and campsites. I guess this will be as good a time as any to give them a try."

"It's getting late," said Mac. "Only the bears can find their way around in the dark."

"Jesus. She has to be out there overnight? What if she's hurt?"

"It's going to be hard waiting, but if you get injured trying to find her, that's not helping anyone. I'll muster the fire department volunteers, and they can help in the search first thing tomorrow.

Mark knows the woods better than most. It may take a while, but he'll find the Jensen site."

Jim ran a hand through his hair. "Do I have a choice?"

"We'll go where you tell us, but I'd say that's a 'not really'."

"Okay," said Jim. "Did you find anything useful here?"

"Sophie's cell phone was in the pool and there is this … " Mac led Jim to a bloodstain near the garage.

"Christ, she is hurt."

"Don't get all fired up," said Mac. "We both know this is not a lot of blood. Maybe she refused to do what they said, so they hit her in the face. It could just be a nosebleed."

Jim put a hand on Mac's shoulder. "Thanks for that. So we'll run with a bleeding-like-a-stuck-pig nosebleed."

"I have a suggestion."

"Let's hear it," said Jim.

"We know Cele Jensen works at the Well Head. We could stake it out and if she comes in, follow her home. If we get lucky, we might even get Jensen. He's not the sharpest knife in the drawer. He might not even suspect Sophie got a message to you."

"Let's go," said Jim, walking towards his vehicle.

"I didn't mean you. You're an out-of-towner. He'll spot you a mile away."

"Who'd you have in mind?"

"My brother-in-law."

Jim smiled. "Naturally."

"He knows what Jensen looks like, and he's proved to be discrete."

"Do it."

· · ·

Jim spent the evening worrying about Sophie. He'd almost given up hope of meeting a woman who, for even a short time, could divert his attention from his job. Sophie was different. She had the same mindset, the same dreams for her life, and the same ideas about what a relationship should be as he did. And while he'd been in a hundred hairy situations in which he'd only had to consider his own welfare, his newly discovered feelings for Sophie gave him a whole new agenda to think about. Imagining her being alone and injured affected him on a level he'd never imagined. But above all , the notion of her being hurt because he'd failed to protect her burned deep into his soul—a soul tormented with the realization that he was falling in love with her, which scared him more than any bad guy did.

CHAPTER THIRTY-ONE

After two hours working on his truck, Rake wanted a beer. "Hey, Cele," he yelled. "Put a chain on Blondie an' let's git goin'. It's payday an' yer owe me."

Cele placed the animal trap cuff around Sophie's ankle and padlocked it in place. Then, putting two fingers between Sophie's ankle and the cuff, she lifted the chain. "See, Miss, it's not so tight an' the chain is plenty long. Yer can move about, go t' the bathroom an' everything. If yer need a drink, it's over there, an' I got bread an' peanut butter in the ice-box. Yer'll be fine 'til we git back. Don't try t' escape or nuthin cos these woods is real dense, you'll git lost. Long as yer do what he says 'til someone pays us, yer'll be fine."

Sophie smiled. "Look, Cele, you seem like a decent kid. Why don't you just leave me the key, and when you're gone, I'll disappear and nothing will be said. I'll tell my boyfriend I went out for a walk and got turned around. Nobody needs to know you took me."

Cele dropped the padlock key in her pocket. "Nah, don't think I kin do it. Need money real bad and you's the best chance o' getting' it. Sit a spell; we'll be back soon enough."

"Cele, yer fat fuck," screamed Rake from outside. "Git out here."

Cele smiled thinly and left Sophie sitting in the kitchenette. "Christ," she said, waddling to Rake. "Hold yer horses. Ya sure about this truck?"

"It'll get us to the Well Head. Won't take me but a minute t' pick up somebody, then I'll have a ride out."

"You'll have a ride out? What about me?"

"You, the baby, an' Blondie. Christ, do I have t' name the whole of creation? Move yer sorry ass. I gotta pick up some tail before they's all taken."

"You're pretty confident."

"Took a heartbeat t' bag yer sorry ass."

"'Cos if yer hadn't, me uncle wudda killed yer. I's underage an' pregnant, even the militia got rules."

•••

When they arrived at the Well Head, the parking lot was crowded with out-of-state vehicles. Rake dropped off Cele and parked a couple of blocks away, in a distant spot in the rear of the Baptist church.

As he sauntered towards the bar, Rake smiled. The church was having a revival, so his truck wouldn't stand out in an empty lot. His wife was tending bar, so he'd get free drinks. As he muscled through the crowd, he spotted several pieces of tail he could snag before "borrowing" their car, never to be seen again. He loved life when things conspired to brighten his day.

Rake didn't acknowledge Cele as she pulled him a twenty-four ounce Bud. He simply sat on a barstool, chugged the beer, and got to see his wife close-up and sober for the first time in a long while. She wasn't, in his eyes, a pretty sight. Before pregnancy, she'd been short and squat, with hair like straw. Now, as her repulsive paunch strained against the flimsy fabric of her smock, he flinched. He hated her bloated belly with its distended button. He loathed her whining and waddling and her constant need for attention. Were it not for her pendulous breasts, and acceptance of any perversion he wished to inflict upon her, she would possess no redeeming qualities at all. Compared to a woman like Blondie, she was a gargoyle. But the overriding beauty of it all was, by late afternoon, he'd be in some other dumb broad's car, heading north with his money and munitions.

"What yer thinking about, Rake?" said Cele coyly.

"Not you, that's for sure. Now keep the beer coming, an' if I hook up wi' someone, I don' wanna see ya fat ass hanging around."

She smiled thinly, and refilled his glass.

• • •

With four beers and no food under his belt, Rake wove his way around the bar. He couldn't remember such a dry spell where women were concerned and now, as he returned to his barstool, even his wife looked attractive. As he ogled her, albeit from her ample bosom up, he thought her marginally acceptable. And as he watched her flirt with guys in the bar, he decided that maybe she should be the one to get them a vehicle.

Then, the unexpected happened. Someone put his head round the door and shouted that someone must have called the cops because the state trooper's unmarked police vehicle was heading into town.

Drunk as he was, Rake knew they were coming for him. Merrill must have made good on his promise and squealed. Rake lit out the back of the Well Head and was halfway down Main Street and ducking into the Baptist church as cops pulled into the bar's parking lot.

• • •

Cele was up to her elbows in dishwater when the cop she knew as Mac walked into the kitchen. And though she said she hadn't seen her husband in a week, others in the bar weren't so willing to protect him. In fact, his unwanted advances on one young woman prompted her to volunteer that he'd just left, heading for Kezar Falls. A policeman took off after Rake in the unmarked car, as Mac pulled Cele aside.

"So, Mrs. Jensen," he said. "It appears you were lying to me."

"'Bout what?"

"Seems your husband was just here, and is now heading for Kezar Falls."

"That right?"

"In fact, he's been here drinking for several hours. I have an eyewitness."

"Really," said Cele. "How would I know that? I wash dishes back here; I don't work out front." At least not when she knew the cops were coming.

"You don't?"

"No, sir, I don't. Not old enough. That wouldn't be legal, would it?"

"And you're all about being legal."

"Right."

"So you maintain you haven't seen him?" asked Mac.

"Right."

"What if I told you I have witnesses that say differently, and if you don't cooperate with me you're looking at a bunch of years in jail?"

Cele smiled. "On charges of what—failure to spot a jackass?"

"Funny. Try obstruction of justice, being an accessory after the fact, and kidnapping."

"I don't know nuthin' about them things."

"Seems there was an incident along the coast your husband may know something about. And a young woman recently disappeared, and we have reason to believe you know where she is."

"He don't tell me nuthin' about where he go and what he do. I'm just around to feed him and warm his bed."

"That a fact?" said Mac. "Well, from what we know, he needed help with a little something that took place here and filtered on down to Boston."

"Don't know nuthin' about Boston."

"What about the disappearance of Ms. Sophie Berg?"

Cele smiled. "Never heard of her."

"Then maybe I'll just put you in the cruiser, take you into Portland, and we can talk some more later."

"Later? You for real? Look at me—I'm 'bout ready to pop. I ain't going no place with any male cop who ain't a certified EMT. You a certified EMT, Mr. Gorilla Hands?"

Mac swiped a hand across his forehead. "I've seen the video and know the basics should anything happen."

"You and your video can kiss my lily white ass. I got rights," snapped Cele. "You get me an EMT, and I don't mean Joey Baloney from some farm who's practiced on sheep and pigs. I want a guy from away, who I ain't gonna meet when I shop for formula." Cele rubbed her belly. "Or I'll take Nelly Lord-Mattson, she's a midwife."

"Then I'll call Nelly."

"Yeah, you do that." Cele knew sending for Nelly would give her time to think. When Rake had snuck home from Boston and hid a bag of money in the woodpile, money she deserved for living with the creep, she'd removed it to a place where he'd never find it. Now she had to find a way to get home and collect it, as well as release Blondie into the woods, before Rake snuck out from hiding and made good on his suggestion to kill her.

• • •

Jim Cromwell arrived at the bar with Nelly, and after a brief examination, the midwife said that Cele was well enough to be questioned further.

He led her to a corner table in the bar. "Mrs. Jensen. Celeste, isn't it?" Jim asked.

"Cele."

"Excuse me?"

"Cele is what I'm called. Nobody save Grampa Hank calls me Celeste, an' that's 'cos he got the Alzymers curse an' thinks I'm Gramma."

"I think it's quite a pretty name."

Cele rolled her eyes. "*Duh*, ya would, yer a cop."

"That being said, let's get down to business. Can I get you something to drink?" asked Jim.

"Why—you wanna get in my pants?"

"Cele, look. I don't know what all hell you've been through, but right now, I'm here to help you."

Cele snorted.

"As you're a local, and nothing is sacred around here, I'll assume you've heard we're busting backwoods meth labs."

"Why's it matter to me?"

"It's only a matter of time before we find your place."

"Said before: why's it matter to me?"

"Because when we do, you'll not only lose your home, but also the chemicals to get you through the day."

Cele frowned. She cared nothing about the trailer, but the meth was another matter. However, once she collected her money, she could quietly disappear and stay dosed on someone else's goods for a considerable time. "Long as I get my clothes and stuff, don't make no never mind to me."

"So let's agree you care nothing about the trailer or the drugs," said Jim. "There's something else a lot more important to consider."

"Like what?"

"The kidnapping of Sophie Berg."

"Never heard of her."

"I know you and Rake took Ms. Berg somewhere, and I also know she was bleeding when you took her. Now, unless we find her pretty soon, and unharmed, you're going to feel the wrath of some very important people raining down on your head."

"Yeah, ain't that just like one o' them Hollywood celebrities." Cele knew she'd said too much and blushed.

Jim smiled. "Thought you'd never heard of her?"

"Seen her in magazines is all."

"Cele, I want you to understand. Right now, you're looking at charges of accessory to drug trafficking and kidnapping. Not to mention assault and any number of violations involving the use of a controlled substance. If you can help us, we'll help you. We can work out a deal. But if you don't, you'll be in jail for a very long time and your baby will spend its life in foster care."

"I have family," said Cele indignantly. "You can't do that."

"As most of your family has felony convictions, you'd be surprised what I can do. On the other hand, if you help me, I will help you. Now where's Ms. Berg?"

Cele remained defiant.

"Okay," said Jim. "Let me leave you a few minutes to think over what I said." With that, he walked away.

As minutes approached an hour, Cele sat quietly, but her anxiety built. When Jim returned, he was grim-faced.

"Well, Cele, it seems your husband escaped into the woods, so you are left to face the music alone. You'll be remanded to the Portland jail, pending further investigations."

"Yer kidding, right?" said a stunned Cele. "I'm underage, near nine months pregnant. I thought the worst yud do is slap me on the wrist an' send me to my aunty."

Jim mimicked Cele and rolled his eyes. "*Duh*, you would, you're a teenager."

"Ya can't do this, I have rights."

"So I heard. They sort of end here, unless you want to discuss it with your legal guardian. That would be your husband, Rake Jensen."

"Sack of shit—useless dick is nothin' to me," snapped Cele. "He just a horny pain in my ass."

"I hear you on that one. However, you are, indeed, under his care. If he means nothing in the big scheme of things, help us out. Where do you guys live?"

"He won't be there. Said yerself he in the woods. Yer won't find him lessen he wants ya to."

"And what about Ms. Berg? Is she at your trailer?"

Cele stared at Jim, but said nothing. She knew from experience that at some point quite soon they'd have to hand her over to her aunt in Cornish. Then she'd sneak back to the trailer, retrieve her money, and release Blondie to fend for herself in the woods. She'd then make her way north to her relatives in the militia. She knew Rake's anger was her fault for not being what he wanted in bed. And she tried so hard to please him because she knew how useless she was. She made Rake mad, but after it all, he could be so sweet and gentle. It was the other times she feared. Without Rake around, she'd could get her thoughts straight and tell her uncle how cruel her husband had been. She could tell them that letting her marry such a snake, just to keep the peace among rival factions, had been wrong. If she timed it right, and set aside her fear, she could escape for good. She would be strong. In the meantime, she knew he was out there and would blame her for everything that happened. Rake always blamed her for everything, and she didn't want him to hurt her. "I ain't got nuthin' to say," said Cele.

"Okay, you've made your position clear," said Jim. "You'll be in the care of the Portland police department until further notice."

"Like hell I will." Cele tried to leave, but Mac blocked her path. "Let me outta here. I got medication; I need t' get home."

"There's only one way you're getting home today," said Jim. "And it's if I take you."

Realizing she was trapped, the youngster's defiance crumbled. She burst into tears, wondering how in hell she'd gotten herself into such a mess. "He'll hurt me," she sobbed. "He'll find me and hurt me."

Jim put his arm around the youngster. "I won't let that happen."

Cele looked into Jim's eyes and she trusted him. Something about him lifted her spirit and made her strong. Despite everything she'd been taught, she believed this cop. And she decided right then and there she wasn't bearing one more consequence of Rake Jensen's actions. It wasn't because she faced charges warranting several years in jail nor because of the beatings and humiliation Rake had inflicted upon her. It wasn't even because she was about to give birth and didn't want her child in the system. She was simply tired. Tired of hiding, tired of watching her back, and most of all, tired of being a victim. If she helped the cops and took them to the trailer, she could at least retrieve her money and climb some way out of the pit in which she'd buried herself. And if she turned Blondie's abduction into Rake's idea and pointed the cops in his direction, he would finally pay for everything bad he'd brought into her life.

"Okay," mumbled Cele. "I'll take ya there."

"Is Ms. Berg at the trailer?"

Cele nodded woodenly.

"Is she hurt?" asked Jim.

"Not much."

"What do you mean by that?"

"Rake hit her with his rifle butt," said Cele matter-of-factly. "Probably busted her nose, but I fixed it good with a band-aid."

"Did you lock her away somewhere?" asked Jim.

Cele glared at him. "What ya think we are? She got a chain on, but she got the run of the trailer, kin get to the bathroom an' everything."

Jim's fists tightened. "How thoughtful of you."

"Why yer gettin' on my case? If it was up to Rake, she'd be dead."

CHAPTER THIRTY-TWO

A caravan of police vehicles snaked slowly through pitch-black woods. And with a trooper walking ahead to mark the trail, it became apparent to Jim why the Jensen campsite had been so hard to find. They were over a mile from the road. Solid stands of centuries-old pines closed around them, and when a fast moving brook at least two feet deep made forward movement seem impossible, Jim questioned Cele's sincerity in leading them to her home. She simply urged the caravan ahead on a line directly toward a pine stained with a logger's "stay" mark.

The first cruiser tentatively rolled into the water. Its wheels encountered a submerged rock-set culvert, and the invisible bridge under the slither of water easily held the vehicle's weight. Once clear of the brook, the others followed.

Vehicles bucked and slipped up a roughly cleared trail skirting a rocky outcropping that brought them to a long-abandoned logging trailhead. It might have taken a team of Forest Rangers a week to find the fully equipped trailer, sitting in the low gully of the century old encampment. As it was, Jim and his team had a guide, and it took them over an hour.

When the lead vehicle pulled to a halt, Jim and Mac got out and crouched behind the cover of its doors. "Jensen, you in there?" Jim shouted. There was no reply. "Sophie, it's Jim. Come to the door." There was no reply, and he ducked back in the vehicle to talk to Cele. "Ms. Berg isn't answering. Is she in the front or back of the trailer?"

"Told yer, she can walk around."

Jim picked up the radio. "Ground teams, spread out and make a perimeter. Keep your eyes peeled and your ears alert. You see Jensen with a gun, fire at will. Okay, everybody, move in."

"Yer can't shoot him without a trial or anything," whined Cele.

"Watch me," said Jim. "Come with me."

As soon as Cele cleared the police vehicle, she realized what she'd done and began to scream. "Rake, run! They's got hundreds of guns. They's gonna kill ya: run, run."

Jim smiled. "Thank you for that. Now we can do our work."

The forest became eerily quiet as Jim, Mac, and Cele approached the trailer. She pulled open the door. "Yer too late," she smiled. "He's bin an' gone 'cos I locked this door."

As Jim stepped into the squalid space, his heart stopped. A length of chain lay on the living room floor.

"Cele, you know me," said Mac. "You gotta help us with this or you're in a boat-load of trouble. Did Jensen take her somewhere else?"

With fire in his eyes, Jim grabbed Cele's arm. "Where'd he take her?"

"I dunno," said the petrified teen. "We was gonna ask for money is all. We don't got no plans to take her someplace else."

"Jesus H. Christ," said Jim, running a hand through his hair. "Mac, take her and the midwife back to Portland."

"Yer said I could—" screamed Cele.

"Shut up before I do something I'll regret. Mac, get going. I'll get a ride back after I look over this pigsty."

As Mac ushered a protesting Cele into his cruiser, Jim beckoned Portland P.D.'s forensic team forward. "Okay, guys," he said. "I want to see if we can get anything from inside the trailer—go ahead and tear this campsite apart."

• • •

In the protective cocoon of the forest's density, there had been no need for Rake Jensen to hide the accoutrements of his meth lab, and a cursory search revealed everything the police officers expected. However, upon observing the impenetrable canopy of the old growth forest, the authorities realized they had no way of airlifting in HAZMAT and DEA teams. It took several more hours for clearance teams to assemble. Then, when lights flooded the area, they dismantled the encampment. Crates were loaded with chemicals, equipment, and meth-making paraphernalia. And they found a stash of money taped beneath the skirt of the trailer.

...

When Jim arrived back at Portland's police headquarters, he spent a few minutes talking to Cele. She had done what they'd asked of her in taking police to Jensen's campsite. However, it quickly became clear that apart from using the drugs her husband produced, she had little to do with his other activities. She admitted to Jim that she shot at Sophie by accident because she had been startled while Rake was poaching a deer. But Jim could get nothing from her with regard to Rake's whereabouts other than, "in the woods." After Cele flatly refused to go to the hospital, preferring to be in the charge of a local midwife, Jim arranged for her conditional release into the custody of her aunt in Cornish.

Though frustrated at the teen's inability to give up Rake and riddled with guilt at his inability to protect Sophie, it was anger Jim found hardest to keep in check. After Cele's attempt to warn her husband at the trailer, Jim wasn't convinced she was even capable of breaking free from her situation. And playing devil's advocate, Jim guessed Rake knew that. Moreover, he expected Rake to come out from wherever he was hiding to find out what Cele might have told the police. To that end, he positioned a police officer in Cornish to monitor Cele's aunt's house.

CHAPTER THIRTY-THREE

Rake woke to the sounds of the forest at dawn. The cacophony of birdsong might have been music to many ears—not so for Rake. He'd have happily napalmed them all. His head was pounding and his anger festered, but as he stepped from the fetid lean-to into the coolness of the forest, the fresh air felt good. Looking about, he recognized he'd brought himself to Wadsworth hide, a seasonal hunting shack alongside its namesake brook. Kneeling beside the crystal flow, he plunged his head beneath the water and let nature deal with his hangover. Instantly revitalized, he shook the water from his hair, cupped his hands, and took long drafts of the forest's icy lifeblood.

It was survival instinct that put him in such a place, and with plentiful water and tools in his truck, he knew he could lie low for a considerable time. Rake smiled. It wouldn't be the first time he'd survived off the land, although he would've liked one of his rifles, and a can of coffee. Nevertheless, he retrieved his tools, set rabbit snares, collected edible berries and roots, and lit a fire. He knew from experience that smoke wouldn't penetrate so dense a canopy, so with a brew of elderberry and dandelion root stewing in a discarded beer can, he hunkered down to wait out the cops.

CHAPTER THIRTY-FOUR

Sophie woke, feeling like crap. It seemed she'd been stumbling about for hours last night before falling into an abandoned campsite and dropping into a deep sleep in the nearest shack. Now, as light began to filter through the trees, she continued walking and encountered a quarry. And she'd been to this particular quarry before—it was the place she and Jim had found the Dodge Ram. Smiling to herself, she closed her eyes and pictured the way back to the road. A few hours later, she was walking up the drive towards Mark Neverson's farm.

•••

"Thank God you're all right," said Jim, when he heard her voice on the other end of the phone. "What happened at the trailer?"

"The chain that gal put on me didn't do much of job. I found some tools, busted a link, and ran like hell."

"How's your face?"

"Nose might be broken, and by the looks of my shirt, I bled like stuck pig."

"Just like I said."

"Excuse me?"

"No matter," said Jim. "I'll be there in twenty minutes to take you to the hospital."

"I guess they should take a look at my nose and maybe do an X-ray because I have a raging headache. And I've got a fat lip and a terrific black eye."

"Why didn't you stay where you were? You must have known I'd find you?"

"I got loose and figured I'd simply find my way back," said Sophie.

"After I warned you about the backwoods? Do you realize how deep you were in the forest?"

"I do now."

"Jesus, Sophie, you could have been lost forever—or attacked by a bear."

Sophie giggled. "Now you tell me?"

"So sit tight; I'll be right there. One question though—how did you know which direction to take?"

" Jim, I'm a pilot. I can navigate by the stars."

CHAPTER THIRTY-FIVE

Each day, Rake left Wadsworth hide to drive the firebreaks and logging trails that brought him within a half-mile of his camp. Then, traversing animal runs only ardent deep-woodsmen knew, he was able to hunker in deep cover yards from his trailer. He quickly noted that the police guards posted there must have been from out of town, for they skirted, but never ventured, into the woods. As he watched the activity, it angered him to see what was left of his possessions, strewn about the yard. However, while he cursed his wife for ratting him out and the police for simply existing, it appeared nobody had uncovered his woodpile stash. He smiled. Useless bastards could all rot in hell.

After four days of intense activity, the police presence dwindled to a single officer who arrived at seven A.M. each morning. Rake supposed he was there to check and maybe walk the mile and a half of ineffectual yellow tape. However, the not-so-dedicated policeman simply pulled up in his cruiser, sat for a couple of minutes, then left. He invariably returned an hour later and sat some more.

On the fifth morning, Rake let his clockwork friend disappear then broke cover and sprinted to his shed. As expected, it was empty, and he moved cautiously to his trailer, also stripped of everything of any value, save some foodstuff in the fridge. It had been off for some days; nevertheless, he wolfed down bread, peanut butter, and a couple of warm Buds. Then he loaded the remaining beer and some canned goods into one of his three military rucksacks and headed for the woodpile.

A cursory look, up close, gave Rake the distinctly uncomfortable feeling that someone had found his stash. He carefully removed the bottom two rows of logs, exposing his buried lock box's metal lid and finding it slightly askew. Cursing under his breath, he dragged the lid aside, revealing the contents of the coffin-sized locker. His munitions appeared untouched and he removed three M16s, two AK47s, a Browning automatic, two handguns, and enough ammunition and incendiaries to start the third world war. They filled his rucksacks and the multiple pockets of the hunting vest he was wearing. Then he reached in to recover his money. It was gone. Cursing the heavens and anything else that might be listening, Rake knew of only one person who would pass on the munitions but take the cash. And he knew exactly where to find the bitch.

With three heavily laden carry-alls, it took Rake half an hour to get back to his truck. Fighting hard to contain his temper, he plowed recklessly down rutted logging trails until he reached the main road. Once he saw the blacktop, his cooler head prevailed. Not knowing who might be looking out for him, he forfeited the ease of the highway and took the old High Road to Cornish.

The closer Rake got to town, the harder it was to check his temper. However, he'd survived this far and wasn't going to blow his escape because of a traffic stop. Pausing at the intersection with High Street, Rake checked for police vehicles or cars he didn't recognize. Seeing nothing untoward, he proceeded sedately to the house of Cele's aunt. Last time she'd covered for him, the cops had released her into the care of good old Bella, so Rake was sure she'd be there.

Making a slow pass, he saw no vehicles parked. Bella only worked when the mood took her, but it was all good. No witnesses to what he was about to do to Cele. Rake turned back down the road and reversed into the neighbor's yard. Leaving the Ford's engine running, he trotted back next door.

There was no give when he tried the knob, and pushing on the door, he found it locked. Nobody locked doors in this part of the world, which convinced Rake his wife was inside. Taking a step back, he kicked hard. As the doorjamb splintered, he burst into the living room.

Cele was feet up in a recliner in front of the TV. But her huge bulk rendered her immovable. When Rake lunged forward and grabbed her by the throat, she tried to scream. She could not.

Lifting Cele by the neck, Rake swung her across the room. "Where's my money, ya thievin' bitch?" he yelled.

"What money?" she stammered, slumping into a chair.

"Do I gotta beat it out o' yer?"

"The cops took it when they searched the place," whined Cele.

"Yer a lying sack o' shit. If they got the money, my stash ud be gone, an' I got that. Which means ya took it." Rake began pulling cushions off the couch. "Do I gotta tear this dump apart?"

"No, they got it, I swear. Please don't do nuthin' crazy," she pleaded.

He'd beaten her before and knew her fear. Her current expression was different. Her face told him everything he needed to know. She was not only terrified but also guilt-ridden. "Yer moved it. That's why the cops got it, right?"

Cele looked to the floor, and giving her no chance for excuses or explanations, Rake dragged the barefoot youngster to his truck.

As Rake wrenched open the passenger door, Cele fought to escape. Her belly hampered her movement. She tried to bite him, and he punched her full in the face. She toppled, semi-conscious, across the truck's bench seat. Rake climbed in alongside her, gunned the engine, and peeled from the yard.

CHAPTER THIRTY-SIX

Jim sped towards the Neverson farm, his mind full of what ifs. He'd had girlfriends before who'd freaked out when encountering the dangers of his job. Even had a couple who'd dumped him because of it. Sophie was the only woman he'd ever met who seemed to deal with whatever came along and bounced back as easily as he did. What was it about the two of them that made their minds so compatible? Why was just being together so important to him? And why did he get an overwhelming feeling of loss every time she flew off? Had he at last found a reason to settle in one place? And if he had, would Sophie want that? And if she did, would whatever they have last? As he turned onto the farm's drive, Jim shrugged off the momentary aberration that was causing him such confusion. But as he spotted Sophie at the farmhouse door, his heart skipped a beat.

Sophie was at his car door when he pulled to a stop. "So what kept you?"

"Had to take an urgent phone call from a battered woman," said Jim, gently touching her face. "Jesus, you look like you went ten rounds with Mike Tyson."

"And you look fabulous," she said. "Come here." Sophie locked her mouth on his.

Jim pulled back. "Doesn't kissing hurt?"

"Don't care, I needed a fix."

"Well thank you for letting me be your drug *du jour*. You sure you're okay?"

"My head is throbbing like an S.O.B."

Jim smiled. "Descriptive and to the point. So let's say our goodbyes to the Neversons and get you to the hospital."

"You know, I probably don't need the hospital. A hot bath, glass of wine, and a cuddle with my favorite Mountie will see me all better."

"Tempted as I am by that prospect," said Jim. "I'll let the X-ray people at Maine Medical be the judge of that."

Within minutes, they were on the road heading to Portland.

"So you navigated your way out by the stars?" asked Jim.

"Sort of," said Sophie. "I was hog tied in the back of a truck, but noticed certain things as they took me into the woods. After I got free, I retraced as best I could until I fell into a campsite. Then when the sun came up, I realized I was at the quarry you took me to. I roughly knew the way back from there and started walking. Next thing I know I'm on the main logging trail which lets out right opposite the farm."

"You know, I near had a heart attack when we got to the Jensen place and you weren't there. I thought he'd taken you someplace else."

"I don't think there was any fear of that. Rake wanted to shoot me. It was little Cele who stopped him. I also think she had second thoughts about kidnapping me."

"How so?" asked Jim.

"She left tools so I could bust the chain."

"It didn't seem she was on your side when I questioned her."

"Really?" said Sophie. "I think that might have something to do with the way he treated her. Isn't there something called Battered Woman Syndrome? The woman knows she's in danger, and suffers abuse, but fear paralyzes her. She'll make excuses for the man she thinks she loves. From what the poor girl told me, she's had a pretty hard life for one so young."

"Now you're making excuses. That's called Stockholm Syndrome."

"What are we doing here?" asked Sophie. "Comparing psychological expertise?"

Jim laughed. "You're a challenge, you know that?"

"I have been told I'm a handful. But on reflection, you seem to be the catalyst for all things perilous in my life. I walk by you in town, I get shot. I visit your cabin and get shot at. I'm cleaning out your pool and get my head bashed in by a deranged kidnapper. Jeezum, what happens next? Do aliens come down and whisk me off to Alpha Centauri? Maybe I should bite the bullet, return to the safety of the big city, and resign myself to a life alone."

"I'm not sure I'd like that."

"The aliens or the bullet?"

"You know what I mean."

"Jim, I've spent my life alone traveling the world and never had so much as a paper cut. I've known you a few months, and I'm an episode of *Criminal Minds*."

Jim frowned. "I get the distinct feeling someone is trying to tell me she's not supposed to be part of this couple."

"Am I wrong?"

"Not entirely. But in my defense, a big part of your involvement in the mayhem is because of who you work for."

"Because you asked me, I stopped flying and I'm about to go stir crazy. It's an addiction, Jim; I need to get back in the air," said Sophie. "I can't stop flying."

"Go work for someone else."

"As a co-pilot? Would you quit being a Mountie and join a city police department?"

"No," said Jim emphatically.

"Then how can you even think I'd take a step back into a co-pilot's seat?"

"Even if it would stop me worrying about you?" asked Jim.

"You're the one chasing bad guys who shoot at you. Don't you think I worry about that? Let's be honest, it doesn't matter what either of us do, we're both driven to careers with risk. There'll always be an element of danger, and we must accept it. We can't prepare for every eventuality. That's not living; that's existing. And you have to live. If you don't, you can't feel. If you can't feel, you couldn't possibly love. And if you never love, you might as well be dead."

Jim smiled. "Wow—where did that come from?"

"Brain is scrambled, but I'm trying to make a point," said Sophie. The women in your past might have relied on you for survival and needed your protection; I don't."

"Well, that put me in my place."

"I'm not trying to put you in your place, Jim. I'm simply pointing out that I can be your friend, lover, and confidante. But I can't be something I'm not."

"I wouldn't want that. I like you as you are. But accepting your fierce independence won't make me stop losing sleep over you."

• • •

Walking into Maine Medical's emergency room, Jim vividly remembered the first time they met and Sophie's reaction to the danger they'd been in. At that time, he was simply a cop protecting her. Now when he thought of protecting anything, his feelings always gravitated to Sophie. He hated to admit she had become an irresistible necessity in his life. That was a notion he'd never before experienced. And though he knew nothing would prevent either of them from pursuing the jobs they loved, it didn't make him any less anxious about her.

• • •

The phone call Jim received rendered him four-letter word spitting mad. It appeared that Rake Jensen had returned to his trailer and removed the bulk of a cache of arms from a bunker under the woodpile. And while he was annoyed at the locals for letting the fugitive slip through the trailer's perimeter, he was furious with the police officer who blew the stakeout in Cornish. Knowing

Jensen had taken Cele captive and was now armed to the teeth chilled his blood. No matter the survivalist's intentions, there was no doubt he was more than capable of killing any number of law enforcement personnel, let alone his wife and their unborn child. That was something Jim could not allow to happen.

As Jim boarded the police helicopter, he could temporarily set aside his concerns for Sophie. She'd be safe in the hospital overnight.

CHAPTER THIRTY-SEVEN

They were on the open road heading for the caves around Clemmons Pond. Rake knew he couldn't both drive and inflict enough pain on Cele to make her tell him what he wanted to know. However, once they reached the remote caves, he'd beat the truth out of her and leave her to rot in the swamp.

He wasn't alone for long. Within a mile of town, a state trooper fell in behind him. And as the vehicles hurtled toward Route 113, the cop pulled alongside. The police cruiser nudged the old Ford in an attempt to force Rake into braking, but the survivalist continued to barrel forward. Nothing interrupted his concentration until he hit the north side of Hiram. There the authorities had positioned a SWAT vehicle across the road. Rake cursed as he thumped the steering wheel. It was clear someone other than the local cops had entered the picture. However, while the troopers might think they had boxed him in, Rake had other ideas. He hadn't hung out with the up country militia without learning something.

Pressing his foot tight to the floor, it appeared inevitable that the old Ford would ram into the roadblock. Then at the last minute, Rake yanked the steering wheel hard right. As his truck lurched onto the grass verge, the cruiser behind him screeched to a halt to avoid a collision with the SWAT wagon.

All the attending officers could do was watch as Rake's truck bucked wildly towards the trees and skidded down the road's bank. Taking out waterside saplings, the passenger side dropped into the drainage ditch. But the vehicle continued to power forwards. Had it been going slower, the drag of the fast moving water might have slowed the truck. But with the engine racing at sixty miles an hour, Rake steered right along the watercourse and tracked around the police blockade.

Bullets zipped past the truck's window and gravel peppered the truck bed as it fishtailed onto the road. Rake fought hard against the wheel and held his line. Amid billowing dirt, the Ford careened onto Notch Road. Rake had made his third escape of the day.

With white knuckles gripping the wheel and jaw set in manic determination, Rake knew if he reached the woods beyond Notch, he'd hit a logging trail and easily leave the cops in his dust. Absolutely nobody knew the trails as well as he did, and it would be simple to turn the most dogged follower around as he zigzagged through the woods.

He hadn't counted on the bitch next to him screaming loud enough to drive a body mad. As he backhanded her again, blood gushed from her nose.

Then he heard the helicopter.

Craning his neck skyward to see how close the aircraft was following, he cursed. It was right over him. But his concentration had to be on Notch Road's hairpin approach two hundred yards ahead. Rake crashed down the gearbox.

As he blasted into the corner with a momentarily unfocused mind, Rake pulled so hard to the left he almost flipped the truck. And as it floated on two wheels, he lifted his foot from the accelerator. The vehicle righted itself. Then he re-hit the gas and blasted down the dirt grade.

Rake saw Clemmons Pond ahead with its caves and surrounding swamp. Beyond there, the cops would never catch him. However, the helicopter hanging hot and heavy overhead would be harder to shake. He knew a couple of local vets who would have tracked him, and could land on a rainforest canopy just for the hell of it. But if the police department's goons were flying this chopper, they wouldn't risk their necks following him near the caves.

As the Ford bucked and bounced, Rake glanced at Cele. She was panting furiously. "Rake, please," she begged. "Stop an' let me out; five seconds is all."

"Shut the fuck up. This is all your fault; yer get what yer deserve."

"I'm sorry. Please let me out. I won't say nuthin'. Please. I gotta birth this baby." One of her hands was wedged against the dash, the other clutching her distended belly. As tears streamed down her face, she began to wail.

As the screaming intensified, Rake wanted to stop and push the banshee that was his wife out of his vehicle. And as he craned his neck to check the helicopter's progress, he eyeballed the bird longer than was prudent. In that split second of distraction, the Ford plunged into deep rough, hit an embankment, and became airborne. With engine racing and wheels impotently spinning, it flew ten feet in the air. It landed in the swamp with steam pouring from the hood.

Stunned but unhurt, Rake sat motionless as the vehicle settled in a couple of inches of muddy water. Then the gut-wrenching wailing assaulted him again. Driven to frenzy by Cele's noise and more enraged than he could imagine, Rake grabbed a pistol and dropped into the murky water. Wading around the stricken truck, he shouldered two rucksacks, returned to the cab, and dragged his wife from her seat. Wrestling the hysterical girl ashore, he headed for one of the Clemons caves used as a hunters' storage shack.

• • •

As Rake viciously spun Cele into the mouth of the cave, her water broke. And as she slumped to the floor, he could see her attempting to push the child from her body. Primal screams reverberated around the underground chamber's walls, and when he could stand it no longer, he struck her with the butt of an AK-47. Blood erupted from a gash over her eye before her head hit the ground.

With silence finally bringing some sanity to his world, Rake found a defendable position and listened for the helicopter. It was no longer in the air. He'd been right. The pilot was a townie who wouldn't approach the caves. Now he knew with whom he was dealing.

Formulating his plan, Rake knew the SWAT team would work at getting to him from the bluff above the cave. Routinely, ground cops would open fire to pin him down as SWAT began their decent and assault. The cops clearly had no idea of the training he'd received, courtesy of Uncle Sam. Even the most experienced of them wouldn't be expecting what he had planned. Moving crates and boxes to act as a barrier and firing stabilizer, Rake set out his munitions.

• • •

Jim jumped from the helicopter and joined Mac and the local sheriff in a defensive position behind a cruiser. Five other cop cars were in place and formed a half circle facing the bluff. Every gun and rifle was aimed at the cave.

"This is your case, Jim," said the sheriff. "You want to take the lead?"

"I think a local may get further with him. Any idea what sort of munitions he has?"

"My spotter says World War Three."

"Jesus," said Jim, glancing around. "Do you have reinforcements coming?"

"Yeah, they should be here any minute."

"Okay, let's see if you can get him to release Cele before the shooting starts."

"You got it." The sheriff's bullhorn squealed. "Jensen," his voice blared. "This is Sheriff Knight. Release your wife and we'll talk."

•••

Calm, resolute, and breathing deeply, Rake cocked his weapon.

"Rake," the sheriff continued. "Come on, son, I'm a reasonable man. Let Cele go and we'll talk."

Rake wasn't about to give up the one thing that might aid his escape. He knew, with absolute certainty, no one would shoot at him if a pregnant woman shielded him. "Tell the Feds to fuck off back to Portland an' we'll talk man-to-man."

"Don't work that way, son. You let us have Cele and we'll move on from there."

"Ain't movin' no place, Sheriff—not 'til the other cops is gone."

The standoff was twenty minutes old when more state troopers arrived and took defensive positions behind their cruisers' open doors. By the muffled noises Rake heard overhead, he knew the SWAT team was in position atop the bluff. He'd trained with the U.S. Navy Seals, and although he'd been dishonorably discharged, they'd taught him enough to ensure he wouldn't go down without taking a few of the enemy with him.

"Rake, Cele's just a kid, and Doc Martin said she's pretty much due. Think about the baby and let her go," pleaded the sheriff.

"She ain't doin' so good, Sheriff," answered Rake. "Needs medical attention."

"You harm her, son?"

"Nah, baby's comin' is all. Yer gonna have to send in a medic; she don't walk so easy."

"Okay, so you put down your weapon, stand to the side nice and peaceful like, and I'll send someone in."

Laying the AK-47 out of his wife's reach, Rake stepped into the cave mouth. He was out of view of anyone above and had his arms out as if in surrender. "Now what?" he shouted.

"Drop all your weapons," repeated the sheriff.

"Don't got no weapons."

"Then come forward, son, nice and slow."

Rake waited until cops began to emerge from their defensive positions. Breathing steadily, he dropped on one knee and snatched a shrapnel grenade from his pant-leg pocket. Pulling the pin, he counted to three. And before anyone knew what was happening, Petty Officer Third Class Richard Jensen dropped and rolled while expertly lobbing the missile at one of the vehicles.

As the grenade bounced off a cruiser's roof, it exploded in mid-air. Rake then hurled a second missile low, which ignited a cruiser's gas tank. Flame instantly enveloped the perimeter, turning the area into a searing hot, molten-metal fireball.

Familiar satisfaction washed over Rake as vehicle fragments and body parts rained to the ground. Moreover, in the time it took for the dust to settle and the cops to regroup, he'd calmly primed an incendiary grenade and pitched that into the chaos. Cries from the wounded accompanied the sickly sweet smell of burning flesh and napalm. And with the fighting odds evened, Rake stepped back into the cave to make his stand.

* * *

Cele was now conscious, with her partially born baby tearing her apart. As indescribable pain drove the youngster toward madness, adrenaline-driven strength surged through her. She launched herself at Rake. Every agonizing contraction focused her anger, and she ferociously bit and clawed at him. The size of her belly prevented her from securing a satisfactory hold, but she locked her arms about his neck and bit down like a rabid pit bull.

When Rake spun in a circle and punched her in the face, Cele slid back to the ground. And as blood poured from her abdomen, Rake hauled her to her feet. She could no longer feel her baby, and an inexplicable strength allowed her to inch him back toward the cave opening. Her intent was to get him in a position where the police could fire on him. But he just grinned at her.

Cele immediately recognized her husband's lecherous look, and a welling of hatred for the evil that he was, flooded over her. She was in too much distress to lose consciousness. She simply wanted Rake Jensen dead. As she lurched forward to push him into an exposed area, her outstretched hand dropped into his jacket pocket. Time seemed to stand still as a bullhorn screamed an order for him to come out or face the consequences. Cele felt the grenade and sunk to the ground, dragging it out.

"Gimme that grenade, ya dumb bitch," yelled Rake. "Ya'll kill us both."

Cele simply smiled, and as blood pooled on the ground between her legs, a violent, uncontrollable surge birthed a small, unmoving being.

"Come on, Cele," whined Rake. "Gimme the grenade, we'll get help for it, it'll be fine."

"It? Our baby is an 'it'?"

"Don't be fucking stupid." He knelt to be level with her, and his face softened. "Ya know what I mean."

Reaching to touch her baby, tears of utter desolation poured from her. "Yeah, I know what you mean." Cele looped her finger through the grenade pin and pulled.

The fear on Rake's face said everything she needed to know. After all the heartache he'd put her through, she had at last gotten the better of the evil bastard. Smiling sweetly, Celeste Abigail Jensen fused herself, her husband Rake, and their stillborn child to the cave walls.

CHAPTER THIRTY-EIGHT

As the volunteer ambulance arrived and helicopters ferried out the critically wounded, Jim and Mac surveyed the damage: five officers dead, two critically wounded, and a half dozen injured. Four vehicles were destroyed and two needed significant repairs. This was the worst day any of the local police officials could remember. Rake Jensen was trash and no real loss to anyone. But it was a sad day when a mother felt sacrificing herself and her child was the only way to save further bloodshed.

Jim held a pressure pad over another leg wound. He'd been in bad situations before, and despite the current carnage, knew things could've been a lot worse.

"Well, Jim," said Mac, nursing a burned hand.

"Looks like the Mounties got their man … again."

Jim smiled thinly. "Yup, that's what we do. But a crapshoot like this puts things into perspective. Makes you realize how fleeting life is, and what is and isn't worth fighting for."

"Whoa, Jim, steady on—that's pretty radical talk for a guy like you."

"Guy like me? And precisely what is that?"

"Lone wolf, committed to the job, single-minded."

Jim put a hand on his friend's shoulder. "Well, maybe I've finally realized that life is about living, and I need something more than this. Now let's get some sutures in my leg before I bleed to death."

CHAPTER THIRTY-NINE

When Jim reached out to set Sophie's overnight bag in the back of his car, he winced.

"You okay?" asked Sophie. "Looked like you hurt something."

"Forgot about the leg is all. Damn shrapnel hit me in the same place as last time. I should just have the doc put a zipper on it."

Sophie frowned. "Last time?"

"Long story—I'll be fine. Now, I promised you lunch."

"Where are we going?"

"I think you might like the Portland Lobster Company."

"God, are you kidding? Their lobster rolls are legendary, and since you're paying, I'm pigging out."

Jim smiled and pecked her on the cheek. "That's my girl."

As Jim pulled away from the curb, Sophie studied his face. She hadn't noticed it before, but he had a scar which ran from his temple up into his scalp. His hands also bore tiny scars around the knuckles, suggesting he'd been involved in more than one fistfight. She knew he was in a dangerous business, but hadn't realized quite how physically involved he became. When she'd asked, he always said, "It's not like you see in the movies," and changed the subject. Now, as they cruised towards Portland's commercial street, an unfamiliar feeling overtook her. She remembered what brought them together and how much mayhem he'd been involved in during the relatively short time she'd known him. Apparently, Jim's life *was* like you see in the movies.

Sophie couldn't help smiling. Her concern for Jim's welfare had become much more than that of a friend. When they were apart, it seemed as if a piece of herself was missing. If she didn't hear his voice, her mind couldn't settle. And when she imagined never seeing him again, a weight of sorrow crushed her soul. There was no denying what she felt for Jim was completely different from any man she'd been involved with. Her feelings for them had been one-dimensional, without depth or sensitivity; the men themselves appeared as vapid, soulless shadows. But Jim was incredibly smart and devilishly handsome, with an inner vulnerability he probably never showed many women. He was intuitive and extraordinarily sensitive and knew exactly what to do and say to make her feel special.

Yet, even as she tried to redirect her emotions, Sophie knew her life was inexorably going off the course she'd set for herself. She had seriously fallen for Jim. *Fallen hard.* And while she'd always maintained that in a relationship, she would do her thing and let her chosen man do his—because it was the only way her independent self could function—that might no longer be possible. She wanted Jim fully in her life. But was she the type of woman who could give up her career for his? Could she be one of those stoic gals who suffered in silence, wondering whether a goodbye kiss might be the last from the man she loved? Could she now, this minute, set aside her concerns and commit herself to him? And if she did, was it what he wanted?

"You okay over there?" asked Jim, pulling to a halt at the lobster shack.

"Yes—why?"

"I can hear the cogs turning. What are you worrying about?"

Sophie smiled. "Your job, my job … just stuff. Being in the hospital gave me time to think."

"Uh oh, that a good or bad thing?"

"Depends—it seems you get hurt a lot."

Jim put a hand on her thigh. "It's a minor occupational hazard. Tell the bad guys to stop running, and I'll stop chasing."

"Couldn't you simply be more careful?"

"I'm always careful," said Jim. "But I deal with desperate people. Sometimes the only way to survive is to be crazier than the crazies."

"And that's supposed to comfort me?"

"No, that's supposed to let you know I know what I'm doing. Now stop worrying. I'm going to fill you full of lobster, and then we'll go back to the cabin, open a bottle of wine, and see what develops."

Sophie frowned. "Thank you, Mr. One-Track-Mind. That puts *us* entirely into perspective."

"Whoa, what's going on, Soph? It's not like you to be so negative. Is this you lobbying for me to give up being a cop?"

"No, why would you think that?"

"This is about the point my girlfriends do."

"I'm not your girlfriend."

"Then what are you?"

"Your *only* friend."

Jim laughed. "Not true and you know it. Darling, we've had this conversation before, and I know the answer. You've made it clear you won't give up flying, and I get that. But Granola is no longer negotiable."

Sophie paused.

"*Sophie* ... "

"Umm, the voice. You haven't used that on me in a while."

"So?" asked Jim. "Have you reconsidered giving up the captain's seat?"

"Why would I do that?"

Jim smiled. "Because you love me."

"Who says I love you?"

Jim leaned across and when he kissed her, she moaned deep in her throat.

• • •

After Sophie dispatched her lobster roll and Jim ate the last of his crab and avocado wrap, the waitress approached the table with a box. When she placed it before Jim, a poorly disguised look of mischief flashed across his face.

"What's that?" asked Sophie.

Jim smiled as he removed an obscenely large piece of Black Forest chocolate cake. Then, from his pocket, he withdrew a large domestic candle and skewered the top of the cake. Sophie giggled as he lit the beacon.

"You look like Billy Monroe when he bought me a cupcake."

"Monroe, eh, do I have a rival?"

"You might have—in second grade. Think he's over me by now. How did you know?"

"It's my job to know," said Jim. "Happy birthday."

"Thank you so much. What did I do to deserve you?"

"This is nothing. I have a gift for you later." Jim felt Sophie's foot slide up his leg. And while that was always good, it was not what he had in mind. "Cool your jets, Captain," he said. "Focus on extinguishing this Olympic torch before we set the place afire."

As Sophie pursed her lips, Jim felt an overwhelming desire to kiss her. He resisted, removed the smoking candle, and placed it aside.

"Can I have that?"

"The candle?"

She nodded.

"It's a big old ugly cellar candle. It was all I had at the cabin. I'll get you one of those fancy scented things with embedded flowers."

"I'd rather have this one," she said, dropping it in her purse. "Says a lot about you."

"Right, that I'm cheap and ordinary and totally domestic?"

"Don't think so, not on your life, and that's what I wanted to hear."

Jim smiled. "Thank you for that. Did I ever tell you we are perfect for each other."

"Don't need to—I know."

He took her hand. "And that we're meant to spend our lives together."

"Don't need to—I know."

"And that you can be a total pain in the—"

Sophie laughed. "Gimme some of that cake." Taking one of the shack's plastic spoons, Sophie lunged into the ganache-covered decadence, making sure a dollop of the liqueur-laced cherry mixture was present. "Do you remember that *Mary Lou's Downfall?*"

"Of course I do," said Jim. "It was the highlight of our first dinner."

"This is much better."

"How so?"

"Because we're sharing it, and I've decided I really do prefer things that way."

"That's new," said Jim. "Is it an omen of things to come?"

Sophie smiled. "You can put money on it."

• • •

As they left the lobster shack, it began to rain. "Come on," said Sophie, looking at the sky. "By the looks of those clouds, it's going to hurl."

"Strange visual," said Jim. "I like rain off the ocean, it's refreshing."

"I'm a pilot; you have to trust me on this one. Five minutes and it'll be torrential." Sophie hurried Jim to the car.

He'd barely closed his door when the heavens opened. "Wow, you weren't kidding; this is *Maid of the Mist* all over again. You ever do that?"

"That's the boat that goes to the base of Niagara Falls, right? Nope, never got there."

"I'll take you there one day; it's an amazing ride."

As wind pummeled and buffeted the vehicle, bursting clouds turned the afternoon to twilight. While the deluge flooded the surrounding area, the downpour was short lived. Within minutes, the rain stopped, the wind abated, and the sun burst forth as bright as ever.

"That was intense," said Jim. "Now buckle up; I'm not wasting another minute sitting around."

Sophie put her hand on Jim's thigh. "Does it bother you when I leave?"

"Of course it does. I like having you around. But I can't make you do something you don't want to. What did we agree to—you do your thing, I'll do mine, and at some point we spend happy time meeting in the middle?"

"Is that how it will always be?"

Jim inclined his head. "Think that's your call. You sure that bash on the head hasn't done some damage? I haven't seen this side of you before."

"Having your brains scrambled makes you see things more clearly. What's going to happen at Granola now you've put all these pieces together?"

"Well, strange as it may seem, it's not easy to shut down a multi-million dollar corporation. With thousands of people's livelihoods at stake, they will be monitored but can continue doing business."

"Even when the authorities know they've done illegal things?"

Jim smiled. "Innocent until proven guilty. Democracy at work. Naturally, I don't expect them to do anything remotely suspicious from his point forward. So for now, we gather our evidence and at some point in the future, we take them to court."

"But you got Goldwater; isn't he Granola's driving force?"

"He was, and we have enough evidence to put him away for life. However, companies like Granola Aviation have layers of hierarchy and contingency plans for every eventuality. We may never actually shut them down. Like a squid, the body loses a tentacle, it's painful for a minute, then grows back."

Sophie frowned. "Doesn't seem right."

"That's the way the system works. Besides, I just catch the bad guys; the rest is up to the lawyers. I can't waste energy thinking about that side of things."

"I agree; you need your energy for more important pursuits."

"And they would be?"

Sophie ran her hand up Jim's thigh. "Take me home and I'll show you."

CHAPTER FORTY

When the limo pulled up in front of the Regent Hotel, Jim stepped from the vehicle and cameras flashed. He tried to move forward but was momentarily held back by the crush. Clearly, Sophie's presence was turning his testimonial dinner into a media circus, and he smiled. If this was what being a celebrity meant, they could keep it.

When he finally maneuvered into the lobby, Sophie was coming from an elevator, and a small bookish young man appeared to be giving her instructions. As soon as she saw Jim, she waved. Then she whispered to the aide, who pocketed his Blackberry and disappeared.

Jim was receiving the key to the city, and the local papers hadn't stopped buzzing about Sergeant James Barton Cromwell of the Royal Canadian Mounted Police. When it got out that his guest at the ceremony was Captain Sophie Berg—pilot to the stars—a whole new level of excitement erupted.

"You look phenomenal," Jim whispered as he hovered over Sophie's cheek.

"And you are positively doing it right," she replied, stepping back to admire Jim in full ceremonial garb. "Now that's the *Dudley Do-right* I've been waiting for."

Jim came to attention, and as if greeting foreign royalty, bowed his head. "Defending the law, ma'am."

Sophie giggled. "Nicely done, Sergeant. Now is your leg going to hold up if I have you dancing all night?"

"I get the feeling we'll be doing more handshaking than dancing. Did you arrange this mob of photographers?"

"Not guilty," said Sophie. "I tried to keep the whole thing hush-hush. I requested additional days off and when HR gave me aggravation, I pulled rank and word got around. Before you know it, Granola's PR and marketing are on my case for a photo opportunity. Frankly, I'm truly sick of all this hoopla, so this is my last media gig for the almighty Granola Aviation."

Jim raised an eyebrow. "So you're going back on the roster?"

"No."

"You're quitting flying?"

"Not flying—just Granola."

"For me?"

"Don't get all smug on me. It simply took me a while to get my head around what I really wanted."

Jim pulled her into a secluded corner. "That's the best news I've heard all day. I could kiss you all over."

"Oh, you're going to, Sergeant."

"So there's hope for us yet."

Sophie ran her fingers down his cheek. "There was always hope for us. But let's not take the spotlight off you. This is your evening and there are an awful lot of people who want to say 'job well done.' Come on, let's face the press."

As they stepped back into the lobby, cameras flashed.

"This is craziness," said Jim. "How do you put up with this paparazzi crap?"

Sophie smiled. "Vanity, sweetie, pure vanity. Now smile for your adoring public."

•••

It was early morning when Jim and Sophie returned to the suite they'd been assigned at the Regent. As she kicked off her shoes and slipped out of her dress, he opened wine from the mini-bar.

"This is the same as your company room," said Jim.

"Very observant, Mr. Mountie," said Sophie, tying her robe around her waist.

"You still nervous about this place?"

"Not with you here. This wine is very nice."

"Okay—so you've quit Granola; not a day too soon I might add. What's going on?"

"I couldn't say anything sooner in case it fell through, and I didn't want to upstage your award dinner. But I've bought the rights to a small freight and charter airline based in Portland. I'll fly daily to all points down the Eastern seaboard."

"That's fantastic; you still get to fly and be a captain."

Sophie smiled. "As well as handling administration, loading, dispatching, and flight services."

"All singing, all dancing; sounds right up your alley. And you'll live where?"

"I really love the cabin and figured if the Neversons will rent it to me after you leave, I'll always be halfway between your home in Canada and mine in Phoenix. And you'll always know where to find me."

"Come here," said Jim, pulling Sophie to her feet. "Have you any idea how much I love you?"

"No," she said, smiling. "I can read stars, not minds."

Jim laughed. "How did we get this far without you knowing?"

"I like the certainty of being told things."

"I'm telling you now," said Jim.

"Good," Sophie replied. "Because I'd feel like a real fool if I gave up everything I've worked for to get rejected."

"Did you really think that would happen?"

"I'm not sure. We seem to have spent an inordinate amount of time pussy footing around."

"Well, no more," said Jim. "If I had a ring, I'd be down on one knee right now. However, all I have is a token *something* I was going to give you when you left. I guess you should have it now."

"Is this a bona fide proposal?"

Jim dropped on one knee. "*Yowch!*" He winced. "Guess my leg isn't one hundred percent, after all."

Sophie giggled. "Jeez. Get up, old man, before you injure yourself. Do I get a ring too?"

"Of course," said Jim.

Sophie smiled. "So hand over the other thing."

Jim handed Sophie a velvet pouch.

"What is it?"

"Look inside."

Sophie pulled the pouch apart to find a gold serpentine chain on which hung a *bullet*. "Where did you get this?"

"You mean after they took it from your shoulder?" asked Jim.

Sophie nodded.

"Evidence room."

"Is that legal?"

Jim smiled. "It's not the real one; it's a gold replica."

"That's awfully extravagant and a bit gruesome."

"If you hate it, I can throw it in a drawer somewhere."

"Absolutely not. I love it and will cherish it as a reminder of how a brave Mountie saved my life." Sophie pressed closer to Jim and whispered softly into his cheek. "I want to hear again that you love me. I want to feel that I'm the last woman you will ever make love to, and I want to see in your eyes that, no matter what, you will always be in my life."

"And you didn't get that already?" asked Jim.

"Not exactly."

"Listen to me, you silly goose." He held her at arm's length. "I have wanted to be with you from the minute I set eyes on you. You are the most exciting, inspiring, delicious woman I have ever met. I adore you, and I can't imagine my life without you. Being apart won't be easy for either of us. My job is almost everything in my life; you are the missing piece that makes life perfect. Believe me, I have never been as committed to any woman as I am to you, and I'll do whatever I can to prove it."

She brushed her lips on his. "So prove it."

Taking her hand, Jim led her to the bed, and with the synchronous movement that comes when two minds and bodies are in perfect harmony, he vowed to always make love to her like it was the last thing he'd ever do.

A Sneak Peek from Crimson Romance
(From *Love Will Find a Way* by Anji Nolan)

The rhythmic beating of wings alerted her, and Emily looked up to see a gull hovering fifteen feet or so above the chaise on which she reclined.

"It's a thief you know," said an accent-tinged voice.

Startled, she turned. "Who's a thief?" She shielded her eyes against the sun, and recognized the elegantly dressed blond from the night before. "Oh hi, Jack Clemmons, isn't it?"

He took off his sunglasses, revealing ice blue eyes. "You remembered."

"How could anyone forget you after such generous contributions to the awards dinner?"

"I'd rather you remembered my sparkling wit and personality."

Emily smiled. "It was a receiving line. I don't recall any chit-chat."

"Yet I remembered the tall redhead with green eyes."

"Occupational hazard, there aren't many of us left." Emily swung her legs from the chaise and retied her pareo about her hips. "So, Jack, I'm guessing the accent is South African."

"You would be correct, and you are American."

She giggled. "No shit, Sherlock, what gave me away?"

"You're very blunt, aren't you?"

"Is that a problem?"

Jack slipped his glasses back on as Emily dug hers from her bag. "Not at all; I like a strong woman. Did you have fun last night?"

"I'd have had more if I'd won the diamond tennis bracelet."

He held out a solid practical hand. "So, come take a look at the bird." Jack helped Emily to her feet, and led her to the parapet. "See the hotel's seafood delivery."

"And?"

He pointed. "Look up there."

The gull had left the terrace and perched on a flagpole across the street. With wings outstretched, it bounced wildly and squawked in agitation as a deliveryman hoisted a basket of seafood on his shoulder.

"Now watch the cheeky moocher," Jack said.

As soon as the fishmonger disappeared down the alley, the gull launched off the pole, and swooped onto the cart. There, head cocked and wings extended, it plucked an expensive tidbit from its kelpy resting-place. It rose high again, and overhead the terrace, dropped its cargo. A large snail hit the ground, bounced twice, and came to rest against the parapet. The bird swooped down beside the mollusk, and tentatively poked the cracked shell to see if its beak would penetrate. When it would not, the hungry flyer danced around the stricken escargot, webbed-feet slapping aggressively on concrete.

Coming from the city, Emily had never seen anything like the seagull dance, and as she watched in rapt fascination the bird regrouped, took the snail back in its beak, and for a second time, rose in the air letting the mollusk plummet to the unforgiving terrace below. This time, a large chunk of shell broke off, exposing the delicacy inside, and before another could swoop in and steal its hard-earned meal, the gull plucked out the spongy gastropod, swallowed it down, and returned to its purloining perch across the street.

"Crafty little critter, isn't it?" said Jack.

"Might say the same about you; how long were you standing behind me?"

"A couple of minutes. I didn't mean to disturb your sunbathing, but I couldn't resist letting you know why the dinner I'm about to buy you is so expensive."

"What makes you think I'm going to dinner with you?" She returned to the chaise.

"Because you said you would."

"Excuse me?"

"I clearly made an impression the last time we spoke."

"And when exactly was that?"

"You don't remember Walvis Bay Holdings's diamond shipment? Last week; you expedited the gems transfer to the clearing house after the courier screwed up. My father, in his usual accusatory fashion, thought the gems had been stolen, and you said you'd make it your mission to locate them before leaving for Monaco."

"That was you? You sound different."

"Last week I was calling ship-to-shore."

"You called me at JFK airport from a boat?"

"My father wanted his gems in-house before he left the U.S. A business colleague said call Emiline Wilks at Transcontinental, she'll make it happen. So I did."

"Your father called Europe from the U.S. to have you check on a shipment clearing in New York?"

"Yup, he called me here, to call you there, to do that."

"Holy Christmas, that's one convoluted chain of command."

"Par for my father's course. He refuses to get personally involved with us peasants. Gets just about anybody, to do anything, at any time he wants."

"You know the chance of anyone stealing a shipment from Transcontinental is pretty remote. Only a couple of us know how to access the vault, and the courier guards have the pickups timed to the minute."

"Doesn't wash with my father; he sees the bad in everybody."

"Now there's a boatload of familial resentment."

"You better believe it. He has me on a leash so tight, I about choke myself. So, are we on for dinner or not?"

"I'm not sure. My roommate is due in today. Besides, Transcontinental really frowns on employees accepting gratuities."

"Female roommate?"

"Something like that."

"Well that clarifies things."

"She's a lesbian."

"And you are … "

Emily smiled. "Not."

"Boyfriend with you?"

"I'm a little old for 'boyfriends'."

"You know what I mean."

"There is someone, back in the states. Is that going to prevent you from taking me to dinner?"

"Don't see him with you, so probably not."

"Then we'll say no more about him and move on."

"Good. And my offer is not a gratuity." Jack pulled up a chair. "Look around. It appears we're the only people under sixty staying at this hotel, and since we're both going to get hungry at some point, why not eat together. It'll be fun, and we can talk about something other than stock portfolios, how much we dropped on the tables last night, or who died when, from what, and left whom, God knows how much money."

"You're staying here, too?"

"No. At the moment I'm a glorified tour guide living on *The Adamas*—that's my father's yacht."

"How exotic." Emily extended her hand. "But a promise is a promise. Hello Jack, my friends call me Emily."

"Well I'm pleased you so generously brought me into the realm of 'friend' and might I suggest dinner at six. Shall I meet you in the lobby or come to your room?"

"Umm, let me think about that … " Emily tapped a finger on the arm of the chaise.

"Oh come on now, you didn't think I was suggesting—"

"Suggesting what, Mr. Clemmons?"

Jack blushed. "Er, nothing. I'll be in the lobby at six." He smiled thinly and walked away.

• • •

Emily saw Jack as the elevator doors opened. And not knowing where they would be going, but realizing most anywhere in Monte Carlo was dressy, she had opted to wear a silk faille two-piece, with Manolos and matching purse.

Jack walked forward and kissed her routinely on both cheeks. "A vision in pale blue. How lovely, Misook, I believe."

"How perceptive. Are you a buyer for Saks in your spare time?"

He smiled. "And the shoes?"

"Don't tell me you know they're Manolo Blahniks?"

"I was going to say, can you walk in them?'"

"What did you have in mind? If you're thinking the Appalachian Trail we could have a problem; but if it's just a turn around the square, I'm your gal."

"Then, Ms. Emily Sarcasm, you are indeed my gal." He proffered his arm. "Walk this way."

She linked his arm as he led her under the cavernous dome of The Hermitage's *Jardin d'Hiver*, and as they stepped out into Monaco's balmy evening air, he paused. "Roommate arrive?"

"Yes, finally. I was in the shower and didn't even see her. She stopped at the room long enough to ditch her bag, and then went to the casino. She drives me nuts with her gambling. She's always working on 'her system' or looking for a cockamamie angle to make money. I'm sick of bailing her out and listening to her sob stories."

"Sob stories?" asked Jack.

"The tables are rigged. Somebody stole my stash. A compulsive gambler's usual excuses."

"Look up there." Jack pointed to a street corner lamppost.

"What are they?"

"Cameras. They are everywhere. The Monaco Tourist Authority brags that you could leave a million bucks in a convertible and if it was stolen, they'd have the thief before he got to the border."

"Well, that takes care of that excuse. What about the rigged tables?"

"Now that's out of my sphere of knowledge; I never gamble. What little money my father pays me is precious."

"Maybe you should meet her and try and impart that wisdom; I'm getting nowhere. In fact, some things have happened lately to make me realize it's time we parted ways. Anyway, I sent her a message at the casino saying I was having dinner with you. And I'm sort of glad I wasn't around when she arrived. Her mood, which is not good at the best of times, will not have improved by sitting in the Geneva airport for twenty-four hours waiting to use her staff pass."

"Isn't getting all psyched up for a trip and being left hanging irritating?"

"For those of us who aren't rich enough to live on a yacht in Monte Carlo harbor, getting a free pass or paying ten percent is worth the hassle."

"Direct, but point taken. Keep walking, Ms. Emily, I can see we're going to get along like a house on fire."

Along with Jack and Emily, many others had chosen to promenade before the impressive Belle Époque buildings of the Square Beaumarchais, and as the smell of coffee and expensive perfume permeated the air, Emily enjoyed the solid feel of Jack's arm, and the way his body fit next to hers.

"So, Jack, what if I'd been a frumpy matron, with bleached blonde hair and ill-fitting dentures. Would we still be going out to dinner?"

"You think I'm that shallow?"

"Just saying."

They stopped at Raffi's, an open air café bustling with patrons. "So, here we are," said Jack, leading her to a table replete with canapés and an open bottle of champagne.

"I see you called ahead," said Emily.

"It pays to be prepared." Jack poured the wine. "Being airline staff, you obviously get to travel anywhere. Have you been here before?"

"First time. This champagne is yummy, and I love canapés. I could happily make a meal of them. How about you?"

"Canapés?"

She giggled. "Monaco; you live here all the time?"

"No, my father has me organize tours for his business associates. This is just one venue for me. I stay on the yacht until it loads up, then I decamp to The Hermitage."

"So that's why you were loitering about."

"I'm not sure The Hermitage would approve of anyone loitering about."

"It is a bit old school,' said Emily. "But I really do like it. I sat in the lobby for hours yesterday imagining all the famous people who'd checked in."

"You know it's stood on the Square Beaumarchais since the early 1900s, and while most people know about Monte Carlo's casino because it has been in several movies, I think The Hermitage is the more beautiful building. Did you know it's a registered historical monument?"

Emily giggled. "That your tour-guide speech?"

"Yup, that's the opening salvo."

"Sounds good."

"I hate it. Standing around, spouting a load of nonsense to people who don't give a rat's ass. It's demoralizing." Jack took a large swallow of champagne. "I'd give my right arm to chuck it all in."

"You work for your father. Tell him you're not happy and want to do something else."

"Wish I could. It's not that simple."

"Why? I'm presuming you're over twenty-one."

"I got into a bit of trouble back home. I'm under court orders."

"What did you do, murder someone?"

"Not quite."

"Uh oh. How 'not quite'?"

"Motor vehicle fatality. Some friends and I got a little drunk—"

"A little?"

"Okay, a lot. You really want to know? My story isn't pretty."

"Stuff that makes anyone as bent out of shape as you appear to be, rarely is. I'm a big girl; let's hear it."

"The trouble started at my graduation ceremony."

"In South Africa?"

Jack nodded. "Cape Town University, I studied international finance. I was valedictorian and me a bunch of friends started celebrating that—and our freedom from school—hours before the speeches ended."

"Okay, we got the drunk driver admission. What next?"

"After polishing off two magnums of champagne, a bottle of vodka and a fifth of gin, we piled into three convertibles and headed for the beach."

"And is that where the bad stuff happened?"

Jack frowned. "You gonna let me get through this or what?"

"Sorry; airline worker, deadlines are a religion."

"With the booze gone, someone suggested we hit The Palms. It's a ritzy beach resort on the dunes, but they refused us entry, 'cos we were all so cooked. And I said 'let's try Nelly Palmers'. It was a ways off, but they'd serve a pickled warthog, if it had a cent. I was the only one who knew the way, so I took the lead."

"When you knew you were too looped to drive?"

"I'm not proud of that," answered Jack. "But we wanted some fun. Needed to let off steam and celebrate our freedom. I admit I was driving fast. But the roads were empty, and everyone seemed okay with it. Nobody said slow down so I hurtled on. Then as I rounded a corner, I misjudged the curve, and ended up fishtailing for half a mile."

"Did you crash?"

"No. But the wall of dust I kicked up wiped out visibility for the guys behind me. I was totally unaware anything had happened until there was an explosion."

"Jesus!"

"Pretty much my thought." Jack took another sip of wine. "As I looked in my rearview, a huge orange fireball was where my friends should be. I slammed my car into reverse and my friend Rick and I jumped out, and the girls with us took off to get help.

"At first, we just stood and watched as pieces of metal shot from the mushroom cloud rising into the sky. We were helpless. Jimbo, driver of the second car, had veered across the road and hit a power pole, which snapped in two. The front of his car was folded round the stake like a giant fortune cookie, and the overhead wires had snapped, catapulting the top of the pole across the road."

"Oh my God," said Emily, hand to her mouth.

"It sliced through the third car, like a cheese cutter." Jack paused to collect himself. "Then I heard a scream. Rick said it was my imagination, but it wasn't. I couldn't see much through the smoke, but I had to do something and stumbled forward. A wall of flame exploded out of nowhere and when I hit the ground, I felt a body. I pulled it from the flames, and Rick who was pre-med, stayed with them as I began to circle the area looking for other survivors. There was another explosion. I recall being launched upward. Then everything went black."

"Jack, I am so sorry. I assume your friends died."

His eyes glazed and he nodded. "Everything was my fault."

"You tried to help; there was nothing you could do."

"Seven of my closest friends died because of my reckless stupidity."

Emily touched his arm. "It was an accident, Jack, one of those awful inexplicable things that just happen."

"Apparently the judge trying my case wasn't entirely of the same opinion. If it hadn't been for my father's influence I'd be in jail now."

"So that's a good thing."

"No, it isn't. Before we left the court, my father not only convinced the judge that to prevent another drunken episode he should retain control over me until I was thirty, but also that I was unfit to handle the responsibility of an inheritance left me by my mother."

"That's not all bad. How old are you now?"

"I'll be twenty-nine in a few weeks."

"So another year or so and you're free."

"It's not that easy."

"I smell a cop-out, Mr. Clemmons. Are we feeling just a tad sorry for our-self?"

Jack smiled indulgently. "I told you, my major at university was international finance. You can't disappear for years and pick up where you left off. Things move so fast, you have to be right on top of trends or you're lost."

"Your life isn't so bad," Emily replied. "You live on a yacht, travel the world—"

"A penniless lackey at my father's beck and call."

"We're all at somebody's beck and call. You just have to make the best of the hand you're dealt."

"Oh, my, Miss Emiline Wilks, where were you three years ago?"

"Let's see; Fiji, meeting Bill."

"Are you going to tell me about him?"

"He was opening a resort and we hit it off after I helped him with something."

Jack smiled. "Much like you helped me."

"Yeah, that's me, the all-American Girl Scout."

Jack took Emily's hand. "I have badges you can earn."

"I'm sure you do, but here's our waiter, so just tell him what you'd like to eat."

Jack grinned and kissed her knuckles.

•••

During dinner, Emily was amazed how much Jack knew about the world, but how unaware he was of the effect his good looks and attentive demeanor had on a woman. The two conversed in bits and pieces of languages they'd learned on their travels, swapped horror stories about lost luggage, and laughed uncontrollably about misadventures with foreign plumbing. They criticized everything about monopolistic communication companies, and the lack of a universal electrical system. And when it appeared a crowd was gathering, and their table was needed, Emily suggested they return to The Hermitage for a nightcap.

Emily led Jack to a quiet spot in The Hermitage's lounge, and a waiter immediately attended them. "Coffee all right, or do you want something stronger?" she asked.

"Coffee's good. I do love how civilized this place is. They really don't mind if you sit all night and just watch the world go by. Now, tell me about the boyfrie—sorry, *gentleman* friend back in America. I assume you argued and are now unattached."

"And you would be wrong. I'm not only here for the awards dinner. I'm working out an issue."

"Oh?"

"Bill and I have the same philosophies, we like many of the same things. But when it comes right down to it, his age gives him limitations. He's a lot older than me; twenty-six years, in fact."

Jack whistled.

"Thank you for that unnecessary musical interlude."

Jack grinned. "Sorry, the age thing was a bit of a shock. Please go on."

"Bill is extremely special. He helped me when I needed a friend. He's supportive, and generous. He has the wherewithal to give me most everything I want—"

"I hear you. That 'most anything' will put a spanner in the works every time."

"You've got some pretty sarcastic notions for a grown man who appears to be completely controlled by his father. What are you, twenty-nine going on twelve?"

"Touché, Ms. Emily, I now have official warning that you bite."

"Sorry, but I've known Bill three years, and he's pretty much everything to me."

"But you're still single, so I assume he's married."

"There you go again. No, he's not."

"Then what's holding him back?"

"He wants marriage, but I'm still thinking about it."

"After three years. Why?"

"Because it's none of your beeswax, that's why."

Jack ran a finger across an eyebrow. "Now I'm sorry. We were getting on so well, I thought we could be honest."

"You're right. If our relationship is so perfect, why am I having dinner and flirting with a virtual stranger? I can only say it's complicated."

"I'm quite good at complicated. Tell me; my shoulder is at your disposal."

"I want kids," said Emily sadly. "Lots of them. But Bill caught mumps at the wrong time and he's sterile."

"Now that's a biggie. Couldn't you adopt?"

"He says he's too old."

"Then I see your dilemma."

"Do you want kids?"

Jack raised an eyebrow. "Is that an invitation?"

"Be serious."

Jack covered her hand with his. "I am. I'm very attracted to you; can't you feel it?"

"You just met me. You have no idea who I am."

"Don't care. We feel right, that's good enough for me."

"Well, Mr. Clemmons, in case you have forgotten, I'm taken." Emily watched Jack for a moment, attempting to assess what was happening between them. She loved Bill, of that she had no doubt. But in a few short hours, Jack had set her senses reeling, had her heart pounding, and introduced feelings that muddled her thinking.

"You know," Jack said, breaking the silence. "Twelve guests can live comfortably aboard *The Adamas*, and the crew is ready to take off anywhere in the world at a moment's notice."

"What are you trying to do, sell me a cruise?"

He laughed. "Not even close, I'm trying to sell you me."

Emily wasn't ready to admit Jack was irresistible. "On such a night with so charming a companion tearing at my sensibilities, I could easily surrender," she said playfully. "Unfortunately, unlike you, my circumstances don't allow me to sail off at a moment's notice."

"Are you making fun of me?"

She held up her thumb and forefinger. "Little bit. So what's the scoop, Jack?"

"I'm not entirely sure what you're getting at," answered Jack. "But here goes. Someone with no knowledge of the impact you're having on me, might suggest that I plan to impress you with my surroundings, and simply maneuver you into a sexual encounter."

"But you're not?"

"Not exactly …"

"How 'not exactly'?"

"Good grief, you certainly know how to put a guy on the spot."

"All part of my charm, dish."

"You're a genuinely interesting person, you've woven your way into my psyche, and I want so much more than sex from you."

Emily laughed. "Did you get that line off a crackerjack box?"

"Was it good? Did I convince you about the not-just-sex thing?"

Emily held up her thumb and finger again. "Little bit," she giggled. "But if you remember, I'm taken."

"I haven't forgotten," whispered Jack. "Don't you feel anything between us?"

Emily chewed on her lip. "How about we get more coffee and you tell me about your family."

"It's not a pretty subject."

"Everybody has a gross Uncle Morty in the closet. How bad can yours be?"

Jack smiled. "You know, Emily, I can't believe I feel so comfortable with you. We just met and I feel like I've known you all my life. What's that all about?"

"It doesn't have to be about anything. Sometimes it's simply two people becoming friends and getting together for dinner and a chat."

"Is that all we are?"

"I don't know you well enough to answer that."

Jack summoned the lounge waiter. "The hell with coffee. If I'm going to spill my guts, I need a brandy. You want some?"

"I'll have a sip of yours if that's okay."

Emily took a small sip when he handed her the snifter. "Our meeting is simply karma," she said. "An amusing cosmic event."

"Don't be flip," said Jack. "I'm serious. What sort of spell have you put on me?"

"I don't need a spell Jack. I might feel something too. But I can keep everything in perspective and not get carried away."

"I've wanted to carry you away from the minute I saw you."

"I know. Now tell me something really personal about yourself. Then, when you get me drunk and disabled, violate my person, and leave me spent and abandoned in the Kasbah, I can point the police directly at you."

"God, I really love your sense of humor."

Jack reached for her hand and she pulled it away.

"Tell me who you are, Jack Clemmons."

In the mood for more Crimson Romance?
Check out *In the Shadow of Evil*
by Nancy C. Weeks
at *CrimsonRomance.com*.